PENGARA SUMMER

Ros Jago returned to Cornwall to help look after her father following his recent illness. She was thankful for the peace of Pengara for here no one knew about her broken love affair. But all was not harmony and tranquillity in the village. She was convinced her father's illness was caused by the trouble-making of the man who had bought her father's failing boatyard. Yet, to her utter confusion, she found this same man extremely attractive.

Books by Anne Goring
in the Ulverscroft Large Print Series:

MORWENNA
PENGARA SUMMER

Love is
a time of enchantment:
in it all days are fair and all fields
green. Youth is blest by it,
old age made benign: the eyes of love see
roses blooming in December,
and sunshine through rain. Verily
is the time of true-love
a time of enchantment—and
Oh! how eager is woman
to be bewitched!

ANNE GORING

PENGARA SUMMER

Complete and Unabridged

ULVERSCROFT
Leicester

First Large Print Edition
published March 1990

Copyright © 1988 by Anne Goring

British Library CIP Data

Goring, Anne
Pengara summer.—Large print ed.—
Ulverscroft large print series: romance
I. Title
823′.914[F]

ISBN 0-7089-2153-1

Published by
F. A. Thorpe (Publishing) Ltd.
Anstey, Leicestershire
Set by Rowland Phototypesetting Ltd.
Bury St. Edmunds, Suffolk
Printed and bound in Great Britain by
T. J. Press (Padstow) Ltd., Padstow, Cornwall

1

ROS shipped the oars, scrambled out of the dinghy on to the crumbling jetty, hitched the painter to a convenient sapling and carefully climbed the old, familiar path to what she and Gwen and their cronies had always called The Lookout. It was merely a grassy promontory with a view across the creek to the village. But in the days when they'd been smugglers or pirates or captive princesses it had served as the plunging deck of the pirate ship where breathless hand-to-hand battles were fought, or the turret of some far-away castle.

Ros smiled, seeming to catch the echo of those childish voices amidst the screeching of the gulls that circled over the creek. The smile didn't quite touch her eyes. Their blue depths were shadowed under the heavy sweep of inky-black lashes as she dropped her bag on to the flower-studded turf and slumped down beside it.

"Take the afternoon off," Auntie Vi had

ordered. "I'll sit with your dad. You get out and make the most of the sunshine. 'Tes the first real sun of summer. My dear soul, you d'need some colour in your cheeks."

Ros pushed back the curly tangle of dark hair from her face. The breeze fingered her pale skin with the softest of caresses. The warmth of the sun seeped through the scarlet wool of her sweater, easing the tension in her shoulders. Almost without realising it she began to relax as the tranquillity of the familiar peaceful scene began to work its magic, banishing the twinges of guilt that told her she shouldn't really be indulging herself. She should be back at the cottage looking after Dad.

"You'll be ill yourself if you don't let up a bit," Aunt Vi had said, crossly, "and what good will you be to anyone then? Now get from under my feet. Have a long walk—or take those paints of yours and do me a nice picture." Her nutbrown face creased into a thousand wrinkles as she smiled reflectively. "If 'tes a pink sort of picture, now, I might fancy it for my bedroom. T'would match my new wallpaper. But nothing too arty," she warned. "Something I can recognise. Not one of your scribbly things . . !"

Ros had managed to suppress her grin until she was outside. Auntie Vi's collection of Rosenwyn Jago originals must be almost crowding her out of her tiny house.

It had begun when they were children. Ros and her sister Gwen had always run to her, eager for adult attention because their father was often too busy to bother. "My, that's pretty," she would exclaim admiringly and indiscriminately over Gwen's attempts at needlework and Ros' drawings. "Now I'll pin this picture up in the kitchen. That nice bright colour'll cheer me up on wet days. And Gwen, lovey, that kettle holder will be a real blessing to me. Aren't you both clever girls, then?"

This last few weeks Ros had been only too glad to sink back and wallow in the comfort of uncritical acceptance. It couldn't remove the pain of rejection—of the last bitter meeting with Malcolm—but at least here, in Pengara, she could relax, be herself, allow the mask of false brightness to slip. No excuses were needed even

3

for being here. Dad had been seriously ill. Gwen, married last autumn, had been whisked away to the States by her American husband. It was only natural that Ros should return to care for her father when he became so ill.

In Pengara no one knew about Malcolm, or her life in London, or about the book which might—or might not—make her fortune. Here, she was firmly embedded in village memory merely as Bill Jago's elder girl. The one who'd gone off to Art College and now did a bit of illustrating or something. Always a tomboy that one. Up to all sorts of mischief, but then what could you expect with the mother dying tragically young and Bill so tied up with his grief and his yard he let the girls run wild?

Perhaps it was some unacknowledged subconscious prompting that had drawn her to this quiet spot, where she really had run happily wild, with all the careless energy and imagination of childhood. Had she expected to recapture something of that unthinking happiness today?

She shook her head wryly as she drew her

sketch pad and watercolours from her bag. Would that it were so simple. But at least she was eager to start painting again. A few weeks ago she'd felt as though every bit of inspiration and enthusiasm had drained from her . . .

She narrowed her eyes against the strong, clear Cornish light. The tide was full and slack, the still water holding a perfect mirror-image of the huddle of houses that was the village, the light fresh greens of the mounded trees and the bold sweep of the sheltering hills.

Down on the quay, the silent boatyard proclaimed "Jago & Sons" in faded Victorian lettering arched over the empty slipway. A couple of yachts swung gently at their moorings. It was a scene she had painted many times, in many moods. She never tired of it, but the inherent sadness in her, in the scene even, communicated itself to her work today.

She lost herself, as she always did once she had pencils or brushes in her hand, time passing unnoticed until she'd finished. Then she propped the completed painting against a lichened stone and shook her head wryly.

"A failure, I'm afraid, Auntie Vi," she said aloud, meaning to add, "Not a scrap of pink in it. More of a blue mood this afternoon."

But a voice, deep and masculine, cut in with an encouraging, "Not at all! You've captured the view remarkably well."

"What . . ." She jumped so violently that the plastic water container, in which she'd been rinsing her brushes, shot from her hand dousing her jeans. The brushes went flying into a clump of budding foxgloves.

"Good grief!" she exclaimed. "Did you have to creep up on me like that?"

"I'm sorry. I thought you realised I was standing there watching you." The voice was apologetic. "I didn't mean . . . here, let me help."

He went on his knees beside her. Together they delved among the broad foxglove leaves.

"There's really no need to bother," she said stiffly, retrieving her favourite sable brush and smoothing its indignantly splayed bristles. The last thing she wanted was an intrusion on her precious moments of solitude. Especially by some hearty ignoramus who fancied himself as an art critic.

"It's the least I can do." He sounded genuinely contrite, but amusement tinged his voice as he handed her the last of the scattered brushes. "This looks more like something you'd paint walls with."

She snatched her beloved hake from him and replaced it tenderly in the custom-made box.

"I assure you," she said sweetly, "that if anyone tried to paint walls with it I'd seriously have to consider kicking him on the shins."

"Remind me never to take that risk," he said gravely. He flourished a large and none-too-pristine handkerchief. "I used this to clean up after I came a cropper on some barbed wire. It's the best I can do, I'm afraid, but it's yours if you want to mop up your jeans."

She eyed the handkerchief. "I don't think that would improve matters."

He chuckled. "Wise decision."

"They'll soon dry. They're old jeans, anyway," she added honestly. "More patch than denim."

She looked at him properly then. She'd

been so concerned over her brushes that she'd only had a vague impression of a bulky shape clad in workmanlike shirt, shorts and husky boots. Now she saw a tall man with a flame of untidy red hair, shirt-sleeves rolled back over tanned forearms, a rucksack on his back. A crestfallen expression sobered sharp grey eyes and a mouth that looked more inclined to encompass laughter than solemnity.

He looked harmless enough, but she just wasn't in the mood for making conversation with strangers. Irritatingly, he showed no inclination to move on.

"I spotted you when I came through the wood," he explained, waving a large hand in the direction of the trees behind them. "I thought you might point me in the direction of the nearest pub."

She pointed. "Pengara," she said. "The Waterman's Arms."

"Nothing at the head of the creek?"

"Nothing."

"Not even a pisky-infested tea room?"

Her mouth twitched. "Not even that." Concentrating sternly she glanced at her watch. "You're too early for the pub,

8

anyway." But she was surprised how late it was. "Should take you about half an hour to walk round the creek to Pengara," she added crisply, "by which time the Waterman's will be opening its doors."

"I've a rare old thirst," he said riffling his fingers through tousled hair which clung damply to his forehead. "I smashed my flask when I fell, not to mention my knee." He glanced down ruefully. "The last few miles have been hard going."

The large blood-stained plaster on his kneecap didn't quite cover an angry-looking swelling. And he did seem hot and exhausted. Ros tried, but she couldn't quite hang on to her indignation.

"Want a lift to Pengara?" she asked, half-hoping he was one of those dedicated hikers who had to slog it out the hard way, wounded or not.

No such luck.

"That would be marvellous," he said fervently. "I hadn't realised the road was so close."

"It isn't," she said. "I came over by boat."

"A boat! My lucky day."

9

"A very small dinghy," she said, eyeing him thoughtfully. "You and your rucksack should just about squeeze in without capsizing it."

"I'm prepared to risk it if you will," he said, scotching her last fleeting hope that he might have a phobia about water or get seasick floating toy boats in his bath.

"Give me a couple of minutes to pack my bag," she said, checking her painting to see if it was dry.

He reached across and took it off her. "I really do like your picture," he said in the same encouraging tone he'd used before. He glanced at it smiling in a polite way that clearly said, "Not at all bad for an amateur." Then his expression altered subtly. He turned the pad so that the sunlight clearly illuminated the strong, clear lines, the subtle depths of colouring that gave the picture an unexpected dimension. He looked from Ros to the painting and back again. "Oh, dear," he said. "Did I sound terribly patronising? You're no weekend painter are you?"

"You did and I'm not." Ros smiled to take the sting from her words, quite

10

unaware that the smile gave her face an unexpected dimension too. She was a girl without a scrap of vanity. Gwen, who took after their mother, had the graceful blonde prettiness that turned every head. Ros had always known herself to be ordinary against her sister's classical good looks—average height, rebellious dark hair that refused to look smoothly groomed, a curvy figure she had given up trying to diet into willowiness. She didn't realise the sudden, unexpected charm of her smile; the way it lit her eyes, drawing attention to the almost sensual richness of the dark blue irises and the heavy fringe of black lashes; the way it revealed an inner warmth and vitality that was not apparent at a casual first glance.

The intruder seemed momentarily to hesitate. Embarrassed at his gaffe, poor man, Ros thought kindly as he stared at her apparently searching for the right words.

"Don't worry, you weren't to know," she said, cheerfully, easing the awkward moment. She glanced round to make sure she had everything. "Right. Shall we take to the high seas?"

"Oh—er—sure."

He tried not to wince as they scrambled down the path to the jetty.

"That knee looks painful," she said.

"Not too bad," he said lightly. "And fortunately it is the last day of my holiday."

"Well, take care on this seaweed," she cautioned. "It's lethally slippery now that the tide's gone down. You don't want to slither off into the mud. You might disappear into it never to be seen again . . . No, I can manage thanks," she added as he made a gallant and somewhat awkward attempt to help her drag the dinghy from where the ebbing tide had grounded it. "I'm used to this . . . there. We're afloat. Now, I'll steady the dinghy if you'd like to step aboard."

"Aye, aye, cap'n," he said, executing a mock salute which she chose to ignore.

Gingerly he hefted himself into the dinghy and sat down. Ros pushed off from the jetty, swung herself neatly into her seat, and let the slow current carry them into deeper water before she began to row.

Almost immediately she realised that she

was sadly out of condition. It was one thing to row herself across at slack water, quite another to row a heavy passenger against the tide.

"As passengers go," she said grimly, hauling on the oars, "I'd have preferred a five-stone weakling. You and your rucksack constitute a hazardous cargo."

"I'm travelling light," he protested. "You should see me when I've got the full works—tent, sleeping bag . . ."

"I'd prefer not to, thanks," she said, drily. "I'm of a nervous disposition."

He chuckled. Sitting as they were, practically nose to nose, it was impossible to escape his direct and oddly disquieting gaze. He sat there, she thought, like Auntie Vi's big marmalade cat—a relaxed, almost sleepy-looking creature, whose amiable appearance concealed a deadly talent for hunting, as many a foolish mouse had found to its cost. Something shrewd and knowing and similarly alert in this man's half-closed eyes put her on her guard. Which was, she scolded herself, quite irrational. Why should it matter? He was merely a stranger, passing briefly in and out of her life.

But, still uneasy, she safely fixed her gaze somewhere above his left shoulder, and enquired with excessive politeness, "Have you come far?"

"From North Devon. Oh, not today! In easy stages. Mostly on the coast path. Staying overnight in small inns and guest houses. Marvellous for recharging the batteries. And you?" he went on. "Are you on holiday?" Then quickly, he added, "No, let me guess. You've got that lovely soft burr in your voice. You must be Cornish."

"True," she said. "But I've lived away from here since I was eighteen . . ." She broke off, making a show of being more breathless than she actually was, not wanting to tell him anything more of herself than she had to. They were in the middle of the creek, passing one of the moored yachts. She hung on to its bow rope for a moment.

"Look, I think I'm going to take a short cut," she said. "Rather than fight the tide to the boatyard, we'll go straight across and land just outside the village." An imp of mischief—long dormant—stirred. "Mind, strictly speaking we'll be trespassing and you may have to brave Snow White's wicked stepmother . . ."

"What?" His eyebrows rose to meet his untidy thatch of red hair.

"'Mirror, mirror on the wall', you remember? The wicked queen? All jet black hair, scarlet lips and evil intentions? Well, you may have thought her a celluloid invention—but she's alive and kicking and living in Kelrozen."

Ros pointed to a large, granite house standing four-square amid lawns and shrubberies that swept down to a low wall at the creek's edge, where the water lapped at an old weedy slip.

"There's a path running from there round to the village. It's a bit overgrown now, and they've put up a couple of fences to stop us poor peasants from using it, but if you're game, so am I. The old bat may not be in," she added, encouragingly. "She may have taken her poor down-trodden daughter on a shopping trip to stock up on vampire's blood and toad's droppings."

He laughed. "Row on. I'm fascinated."

"You might well be," Ros said dourly, glad to have diverted his attention away from herself. "You don't have her as a neighbour. She really is a pain in the neck —not to mention the wild friends she has down for the occasional orgy."

"You're joking!"

She grinned and pulled hard on the oars. "Well, allowing for a modicum of exaggeration—you know how it is in a small place—I hear there were some noisy parties up there this winter. And Porsches and Mercs and Jags cluttering the lanes and revving up in the small hours don't exactly make for good public relations."

"Tell me more!"

As she'd expected, the current was slacker here. Just a few more minutes and she could see her passenger on his way.

"More? I couldn't bore you with all the grisly details, it'd take a week," she said lightly. "Suffice to say she guards that property—which isn't even hers—as fiercely as a dragon whose diet of virgins has been withheld." She manoeuvred the dinghy to the foot of the slip. "Which probably gives you some idea of the character of the man who's actually installed our dear Dolores as caretaker."

"Oh? Who's that?"

"Paul Burford." She couldn't help it. Bitterness underlined each syllable. Damn. She shouldn't have brought his name into the conversation. She climbed out of the dinghy. Her passenger didn't move.

"I take it," he said, "that he isn't exactly your favourite person."

"I've never met him," she said stiffly.

"Sounds as though you don't want to."

"Right."

Fiercely she hitched the painter to a ring in the wall.

"I'll show you the path and come back later for the dinghy . . ."

"You look as though you wish you were tying that rope round the poor man's neck." He sounded amused. "What has he done to you?"

She tightened her lips. "It's no laughing matter," she said, wanting to wipe that enigmatic, mocking look off his face. The words formed themselves in her head, then they spilled out, almost without volition. "Paul Burford ruined my father and almost killed him."

To her mortification her voice wavered unsteadily, as though putting her unspoken thoughts into words had released the hurt and worry she'd been suppressing for so long. She swallowed hard and shot the stranger a quelling look that said, "Don't you dare ask me another personal question!" Then she stalked back to the dinghy and yanked out her bag. "Now, are you going to sit there all day? I have work to do if you haven't."

He stared at her in silence. The amusement had quite gone from his face, replaced by some other, less readable, emotion. Without the smile his face looked harder, older. Not so much dozey marmalade cat, she thought, as tough, battle-hardened lion. But to her relief he stood up meekly and stepped out of the dinghy.

She'd forgotten to remind him of the dangers underfoot. The moment his boots hit the slimy green weed they skidded alarmingly.

Ros grabbed him. Together they executed a wild flailing dance as they fought for balance, clinging on to each other. Presently they came to a breathless halt and he murmured above her head, "Do you come here often? The band's great but the floor's a disgrace. I shall complain to the management."

She couldn't help herself. Giggles rose like bubbles into her throat. Impossible to suppress them. And even as her laughter burst out to join his throaty roar she found herself surprised to hear it. It seemed ages since she'd found anything to laugh about.

A startled blackbird foraging above the tide line flew off chattering in alarm. Odd really, Ros thought, that a stranger should be the one to trigger off a moment of pure emotional release . . . What wasn't so odd, she realised, sobering swiftly, was that he was reckoning on taking advantage. He still had his hands on her shoulders. And those hands showed no inclination to let go. His grey eyes were intent. He said softly, "I don't even know your name."

"It doesn't matter, does it?" she said brightly.

"But it does. Very much."

She tried to shrug off his hands. His grip remained firm.

"Once you're on your way, our paths are hardly likely to cross again," she protested.

"That's where you're wrong," he said. "You see I have a . . ."

"What is this?" The loud commanding voice sliced between them. "What are you doing here?"

"Oh, help," Ros whispered. "The dreaded Dolores."

"This is private property! I have told you people more than once. It is written here for all to see." She stood above them on the sea wall, pointing a dramatic finger to the raw new noticeboard impaled on the edge of the lawn. "But you do not read. And if you do you choose to disregard it . . ."

"I do see what you mean." The words slipped softly into Ros' ear. "She could play the part of the Wicked Queen beautifully, couldn't she?"

She was a tall, full-bosomed woman, her glossy black hair drawn back into swooping wings which emphasised her white skin and large, dark, angry eyes. The scarlet of her lips and nails was matched exactly by the flowing red dress which blew around her in the breeze like billowing regal robes. She was a magnificent and melodramatic figure. And, having gained the stage—even if it was merely a sea wall—seemed in no way inclined to leave it before she'd delivered a full speech in her heavily accented English.

". . . time and again," she anguished, "I find prowlers sneaking through my grounds. And now, it is two people making love together practically under my nose . . ."

"What?" Ros gasped, embarrassed colour rushing to her cheeks.

". . . It is quite intolerable. I shall call the police if you do not instantly remove yourselves!"

Ros wriggled energetically out of the red-haired man's embrace. "That's ridiculous! We were only . . ."

Before she could launch into an explanation, the slender girl who'd drifted into view behind Dolores suddenly gave an excited cry, then hurtled down the slipway.

"Paul!" she cried. "Oh, Mother, it's Paul."

Ros' jaw dropped. She watched the man pick up Dolores Partington's daughter and swing her round, laughing. She clung to his neck, long fair hair flying wildly, pouring out a torrent of questions. "Where did you pop up from? Did you have a lovely holiday? Why didn't you tell us you'd be here today . . ?"

Then Dolores was moving majestically towards them, scolding, holding out her hands.

"Paul, it is very naughty of you to spring yourself on us—and so scruffy you look! No wonder I mistook you for a trespasser." She plonked an energetic kiss on his right cheek then his left and tucked her arm in his. Her daughter happily hung on to the other. "Come along to the house. You must be exhausted, all that striding about the countryside when you could have been having a restful time here in your own home with Tania and I to look after you."

"In a moment, Dolores," he said and his smile faded as he turned to look at Ros.

She still stood there, motionless, the colour draining from her face.

"You're Paul Burford," she said faintly.

"Afraid so," he said. "I did try to tell you . . . Come up to the house. We must

22

talk . . ." He spoke quickly and urgently, but she didn't stop to listen.

She turned her back, fled to the dinghy, unhitched it and flung herself on board.

For a moment he watched her as she began to row with fierce swift strokes, steadily widening the gap between them.

It seemed as if he might call after her, but then he shrugged, shook his head, and turned his attention to the two women who had welcomed him so warmly, and began to walk with them towards the house.

2

AUNTIE VI was pulling on an enveloping brown cardigan as Ros pushed open the sitting-room door.

"Here she is now," Auntie Vi said. "Told you there was nothing to worry about, didn't I, Bill?" She winked at Ros. "Getting into a right old fusspot, he is. Had you drowned in the creek or lying with your leg broken somewhere."

"I . . . I lost track of the time," Ros said breathlessly.

"Don't you worry none, m'dear." Auntie Vi eased her comfortable bulk into the narrow hall. "Nothing for you to rush back for. I put that casserole in the oven like you said so your dinner's nearly ready. Oh, and there was a phone call for you. From one of your London friends."

Ros' stomach gave an involuntary lurch. Malcolm?

"Susie she said her name was."

Of course it wouldn't have been

24

Malcolm. He didn't know—or care—where she was.

"Said to be sure to phone her tonight. Something she wants to ask you about urgent."

When the door closed on Auntie Vi's cheerful promises to look in again tomorrow the room seemed suddenly very quiet and still, despite the soft crackle of logs burning in the fireplace.

Coming in from the fresh air, the room felt unbearably overheated to Ros, but her father was hunched as usual over the fire, a rug across his knees as though it were midwinter.

Ros felt a pang of love and sadness. He was so thin and gaunt, his unruly hair—so like her own in texture and colour—now heavily streaked with grey. He looked what he was, a defeated man. Fifteen years ago, when his wife had died, he'd had his beloved boatyard to turn to. Work had been his salvation. Now the yard was gone, along with his robust health. Everything had come to an end for him. And nothing that the doctor or Auntie Vi or Ros said or did could seem to jolt him out of the limbo of depression into which he had drifted.

Ros chattered cheerfully as she whisked about seeing to the meal and setting the table. Her father answered in monosyllables. Only when she showed him the picture she'd painted that afternoon did any animation come into his face.

He studied the picture for a long time then, his eyes still on the painting, he said gruffly, "I've never said it before, Ros, but I want you to know I'm proud of you."

"Oh, Dad." Ros laid her hand on his shoulder.

"Never gave you much encouragement, did I?" he went on. "Thought it was a lot of airy-fairy nonsense you wanting to go off to Art College. Remember the arguments?"

"Do I!"

"I wanted you to learn shorthand and typing and get yourself a nice secretarial job in Truro or Falmouth. Seemed a proper sort of a career, that did. Painting and drawing was something you could play at in your spare time."

"Not for me," she said simply. "It was

—well—it was the only thing I knew that I could be good at." She laughed. "I'd have made a rotten secretary."

"Far too independent and stubborn, that's for sure," he growled and for a moment the old twinkle glinted in his eye. "Like your old man." Then his face settled back into its recently acquired lines of dour resignation. "I'd have done things differently if I had my time again. Helped you two girls. Given you more attention. Not left your welfare so much to other people. But you know how things were after your mother died. Couldn't seem to think straight . . ."

"Don't, Dad," Ros said quickly. "You did the best you could for us."

"Like I said . . . you—and Gwen—a man couldn't wish for better daughters." He cleared his throat in an embarrassed way. "And I'm glad you're here, Ros. That's all I wanted to say."

He had always been a man who scoffed at soft words and displays of emotion. Ros knew just how much that statement had cost him. She swallowed hard, patted his shoulder and dropped a quick, light kiss on his rough hair before she went back to the kitchen.

After they'd eaten she rang Susie. She dialled the number, picturing the phone ringing in the narrow Victorian house she shared with three other girls—her home and work base for the last two years since she'd taken the plunge into freelance illustration.

"Ros! Hang on a minute . . . terrible racket. Lynn's celebrating. She's landed that fashion buyer's job she was after." Susie took the phone from her ear and yelled. A door banged, cutting off the background blur of music and voices. "That's better," she announced. "Now I can hear myself think." She sounded breathless. "Pity you're in darkest Cornwall, love. Looks like being a lively evening."

Ros could imagine.

"Wish I was there," she said, a little wistfully.

"Things not so good, then?"

"Improving." "I think," she added silently to herself. "It's a slow job."

"Bound to be," Susie said sympathetically. "I gather you won't be back just yet."

"I'll have to give Dad another week at least."

"That was what I was ringing about actually. There's a new girl in the pharmacy, living miles out. She's having trouble getting digs locally and I wondered . . ."

"Be my guest," Ros cut in. It was an understood arrangement that friends could be put up temporarily if any of the resident girls was away. "She'll probably have to hack through paper and canvas to get to bed. I did leave in rather a hurry."

"I'll have a tidy round," Susie assured her. "You're a doll, Ros. And I'll put your studio out of bounds. I know you won't want her straying in there . . . Oh, and talking of work, there's some post accumulating, including a couple of parcels. Want me to readdress it all?"

"Please."

"Managing to get any work done down there?"

"A little. Finished a couple of commissions. Should keep the wolf from the door until I'm back in circulation . . ."

29

They chatted on for a few moments catching up on the news, but when Ros finally put down the phone, she stayed hunched on the chair as though reluctant to dispel the last echoes of Susie's cheerful gossip. A stray spear of evening sun angling down from the fanlight over the front door spotlit the muddy hem of her patched jeans and the scuffed toe of her trainers. Lynn, she thought with a smile, definitely wouldn't approve. She'd worked in the rag trade for years and was forever hurling advice—not to mention her expensive cast-offs—at her friends. And they'd all be dressed up to the nines tonight in Lynn's honour. The house would be full of people and laughter and thumping music.

"You finished on the phone?" Her father had come to the sitting-room door and was frowning at her anxiously. She knew the question he longed to ask but couldn't.

She summoned up a reassuring smile. "Susie just wanted to put a new colleague from the hospital in my room for a few days."

"So you'll be staying a bit longer?" The relief on his face was clear to see.

"You don't get rid of me that easily." She stood up briskly, dispelling the pangs of nostalgia for her friends and her London world. "Now, how about a drive? You haven't had your exercise today. I could run you up to The Beacon and we could walk a little way on the cliff path."

He shook his head.

"You know what the doctor said," she scolded. "Walking's good for you as long as you take it easy and avoid steep hills."

"Oh, I'd like to go out," he said to her surprise, for she usually had practically to frog-march him across the doorstep. "I'd like to walk as far as the boatyard."

"Oh, Dad," she said softly. "Are you sure? Won't it be too upsetting?"

A bleak smile touched his lips.

"I'll have to face it some time, girl. I can't go round with my eyes closed. And it's tomorrow they start pulling it to bits, isn't it? I'd like to have one last look at the old place."

It was a slow walk because the balmy evening air had drawn most of Pengara out

31

of doors. Bill Jago was stopped time and again with solicitous enquiries about his health and a barrage of well-meaning advice as they wound their way from their cottage. By the time they'd negotiated the knot of people chatting on the corner by the general shop-cum-post office, the crowded benches set outside The Waterman's Arms and the strollers along the quay he was beginning to get edgy. After a lengthy encounter with old Mrs. Salter taking the sun on a chair outside her front door between foaming tubs of pink geraniums, he had become monosyllabic, leaving Ros to do all the talking.

"Anyone'd think no one had ever been ill before," he grumbled when they finally tore themselves away. "Keeping me hanging about while they tell me about remedies that their old grandad swore by."

"They care about you, Dad," Ros protested gently.

"But boiled nettles and dry chestnuts! I've got enough pills and potions from the doctor without poisoning myself with that rubbish . . ." He broke off, his face darkening, as a metallic blue saloon car bounced towards them.

The cobbled road ran between a terrace of stone-built cottages and the low wall that fringed the creek. Few local drivers used it as it was only wide enough to take one car and there was a safer, smoother road to the boatyard higher up the hill. The driver of the blue saloon obviously had no qualms—and no intention of slowing for strollers. Hooting the horn impatiently, he swept past them looking neither to left nor right.

"You saw who that was?" Bill said grimly, watching the saloon round the corner into Fore Street. "That nasty piece of goods Burford uses to do his dirty work. Langley. Been down to the yard to have a good gloat, I dare say."

Ros sighed. The omens were definitely inauspicious. She wished they'd gone up to The Beacon. She couldn't think that anything good would come of this visit except to depress Dad's spirits further. Besides, the glimpse of the smooth and silvery-tongued Mr. Langley, who'd been a thorn in Dad's side for so long, reminded her inevitably of her encounter with his boss. She had deliberately pushed all thoughts of him firmly into the deepest recesses of her mind. Now, unbidden and unwanted, his image swam into her head. She saw him, big, relaxed, smiling but with the shrewd, sharp look in his eyes that had set her on her guard. When she'd found out who her passenger really was unease had given way to shock and anger. Now the anger had settled to a deep hostility and a strong desire not to encounter him again. If Mr. Langley had been at the yard it was possible Paul Burford might be hanging around there too. And what that would do to her father's blood pressure she could well imagine.

But the man standing staring round at the locked and silent buildings, at the rusty winches, abandoned boat cradles, blocks and props lying amid the encroaching weeds—the detritus of a century of activity—was familiar and unthreatening.

"It's young Jason Penrose," Bill said, surprised.

"So it is," Ros said with relief as he waved and came to meet them.

She'd been at school with Jason. He'd left Pengara to embark on his architectural training at the same time as Ros. She'd seen him occasionally over the years when their flying visits home had coincided. He'd been a shy, studious child and had grown to a stocky, serious young man with a pleasant, diffident manner.

"I hadn't heard you were back," she said when the greetings were over.

"I only got here today," he said, an uneasy expression clouding his face as he looked from Ros to her father. "I . . . that is . . . I have to be frank with you, Mr. Jago. I'm involved with this." He gestured at the buildings. "I've designed the new complex for Paul Burford."

Bill stared at him as though he'd been struck.

"I understand how you must feel," Jason went on earnestly. "It must hit hard when an old family business has to be sold. But change is inevitable sometimes." Into the taut silence he added, "Paul wanted an architect with local connections and believe me, I've done my damndest to design something that will be worthy of the village and the area. It'll incorporate the best of the old and . . ."

"A leg up for you, eh?" Bill said

heavily. "Working for someone influential like Burford."

"I can't deny it," Jason said quietly.

Bill shook his head and stared round at the place that had been his little empire for so long.

"And I can't blame you, boy," he said after a long moment. He straightened his shoulders as though coming to a decision. "Well, seeing as you're here, you might as well tell me the worst. What havoc are you proposing to wreak on the old place?"

Ros let out her breath, thankful that her father was keeping calm. He'd always liked Jason. She could think of no one better to smooth over this potentially difficult moment—or to have designed the new buildings. At least he had the interests of the village and its people at heart. Perhaps that knowledge would bring Dad some comfort.

She watched the two of them as Jason enthusiastically pointed and gestured, outlining his plans. When they wandered into one of the old open-sided boat sheds she drifted away on her own farewell tour.

It was hard to believe how busy and

productive the yard had been in its heyday. Her great-grandfather had started the business, employing his two sons then, in turn, their sons. But two world wars, the lure of distant, livelier places had done their work. Out of all the Jago family who'd once thrived in Pengara, only Ros and her father were left—and she was just a visitor nowadays.

It wasn't only the long blue evening shadows that made her shiver and hug her arms and move quickly to the back of the solid granite building that had once been the heart of the yard. She stopped at the small sash window, thick with cobwebs and ancient sawdust, that had never closed properly, forced it upwards and climbed in.

She was at the back of the main workshop. Here Jago's tough wooden clinker-built dinghies and launches had been built. Now, the dank emptiness echoed back the sound of her footsteps as she crossed to the stairs and climbed to the upper floor.

She found what she was looking for at the end of the passage. The door creaked rustily as she pushed it open to reveal a small cubbyhole with a window over-looking the creek, empty except for a rough shelf holding a drift of dusty papers. She picked them up then froze, her breath catching in her throat, at the sound of a soft footfall moving along the passage.

She turned quickly, forgetting about the dust, clutching the papers to her chest as though for protection.

Paul Burford stood in the doorway, smiling lazily.

"Well, well," he said softly. "A burglar no less."

In the confined space he looked taller, bigger and more formidable than she remembered. Gone was the tousled friendly hiker. The red hair was damply sleek as though he had just emerged from a shower. He wore casual—expensively casual—grey slacks and jacket and a pale blue silk shirt. She caught the tang of his spicy aftershave as he moved a step nearer.

"So what are you stealing?" he enquired. "Secret plans of some diabolical weapon that will blow Burford Enterprises to smithereens?"

"Don't be ridiculous." She found her voice; managed to inject into it just the right note of scorn. "Here." She thrust the papers at him. "See for yourself."

He riffled through them. She saw, with satisfaction, the smear of dust that had lodged on one immaculate cuff. He glanced up at her, his mouth quirking with amusement.

"Early efforts I gather. I do like the animal. A sort of smiling hairy cube on four table legs."

"A dog we used to have," she said, scowling.

"It has . . . promise," he said gravely.

"I was only five or six when I painted that," she protested.

"And what are these Rosenwyn Jago masterpieces doing here?"

She gestured round. "This was my first studio. Dad used to bring Gwen and I here to give my mother a rest—she wasn't strong, you see." She broke off, frowned. "So you know my name?"

"Not difficult to find out in a place this size."

"Then you know why I said . . . what I did."

"That I ruined your father? Almost

killed him? The words are engraved on my heart."

"It isn't funny," she said icily.

"Who's laughing? I'm only repeating what you told me. If it sounds histrionic you've only yourself to blame."

"It's true!" she burst out. "If it wasn't for your conniving and . . . pressure, Dad wouldn't have had to give in and sell to you. And he wouldn't have had that ghastly heart attack after all the worry and upset."

For a big man he moved very quickly. His hand shot out and grabbed her wrist. He pulled her towards him with a rough jerk.

"Let me go! You . . . you oaf."

"Not until you explain yourself."

"Explain! You must know very well what you did."

"What I did," he said very slowly and clearly, "was to fall in love with Pengara. Is that so wrong? I bought a house. I saw a boatyard that was clearly in a parlous state and that had possibilities for development—for bringing new life to the heart of the village."

"And you were determined to get that boatyard at any cost."

"I put in a bid for it."

"And when it wasn't accepted, you set about making sure my father had no option but to sell."

His grip on her wrist didn't slacken. She was forced to stand very close to him, so close that she could see the tawny flecks in his grey eyes; and the puzzled look that momentarily clouded them.

"You set that slimy character Langley on to him," she said fiercely. "He made Dad's life a misery, he bullied, cajoled, threatened . . ."

"Threatened!"

"Nasty little hints insinuated into the conversation. If Dad wouldn't sell, then Langley would make damn sure he'd have no business left to sell."

"I don't believe this! Langley worked for my cousin for years . . ."

"Huh! That doesn't say much for your cousin. Langley certainly set about matching his sly hints with effective actions."

"Such as?" He seemed—he sounded— genuinely taken aback.

"Such as removing the one customer Dad was relying on to see him through a bad patch. He'd ordered two dinghies which would have kept the yard ticking over during the winter. But the order was cancelled." She stared at him unflinchingly. "Another boatyard down the coast had undercut Jago's prices by an absolutely ridiculous amount. Dad couldn't possibly compete. We learned later that Langley himself had bought an interest in this other yard and was busily turning it into one of those flashy marinas where jaded businessmen keep their gin palaces. Not hard to put two and two together, is it?"

Into the silence came the little rustlings of draughts, the soft plop of water from a distant leaky tap.

"Langley had done his homework well. Dad's life savings were all tied up in the business. His creditors were pressing. There was no way out for him but to sell up. His health started to deteriorate from the time he signed the papers. Two months ago he had a heart attack." Her voice was level, unemotional. "His heart was broken in more ways than one, Mr.

Burford. Now you can, perhaps, see why I spoke as I did."

He was still holding her wrist. Loosely now, absently, staring over her head through the dusty glass to where the water lapped in, calm and serene, over the muddy creek bed. Then, slowly, his gaze came back to her.

"Never apologise, never explain," he said softly. "That's what they tell you, isn't it? Well, I'm going to do both."

"A bit late in the day," she said in the same flat tone.

"Nevertheless, I am sorry. If what you tell me is the truth—and I've no reason to believe otherwise—then Langley's behaviour is both despicable and inexcusable." His gaze was unflinching. "You see I've been out of the country for most of the last year settling up my affairs in New Zealand . . ."

"Leaving Burford Enterprises to its own nefarious devices?"

"It was my cousin's business," he went on, ignoring her interruption. "He was a good deal older than me and he never married. He died suddenly two years ago —and it was the biggest shock of my life to find I was his heir." He sounded genuinely amazed. "I mean, I'd only met him a few times when I was a child. Then he used to invite me to the occasional slap-up meal when I was an impoverished undergraduate. I'd hear nothing for months in between. Never even a Christmas card after I joined my parents who'd moved to New Zealand—until the thunderbolt came from the solicitors."

"And turned you into a multi-millionaire overnight."

"Hardly," his quick grin flashed out. "But a whole deal richer than any other civil engineer of my acquaintance." His grin faded. He looked almost gloomy for a moment. "It was one hell of a prospect, and I wasn't sure I wanted to take it on. Board meetings, desk work, all that high-powered tycoon stuff . . . I was perfectly happy in New Zealand."

She had to give him his due, he was a darned good actor. Either that or . . . No, she couldn't—wouldn't—let herself be conned into believing that he was sincere.

"You could have sold out, couldn't you?" she said coolly.

"Ah, but I have one terrible flaw in my

character." His eyes mocked her. His fingers, locked lightly round her wrist, stirred warmly against her cool skin as though seeking the pulse that beat there. "I never can resist a challenge."

She wrenched her hand away, took a couple of steps backward so that she fetched up against the shelf.

"I think I've stood here long enough listening to your . . . your excuses." She said the first thing that came into her head. Wanting, suddenly, to get out of this claustrophobic airless room that reeked of age and decay. "If you'd move out of the way?"

But he still stood there, leaning on the doorpost, arms folded.

"Don't you want to hear how I came back to England to see if I could possibly settle? How I'd forgotten how green and cool and beautiful England was? How I came to Pengara and saw Kelrozen waiting all forlorn for me to rescue her from the ravages of dry rot and woodworm?"

"You have an imaginative turn of phrase, Mr. Burford."

"But you still believe I was involved in Langley's little game?"

"Yes!" Then, after a pause in which she wrestled with her conscience, honesty compelled her to say, "Well, I . . . that is . . . you make out a convincing case." She glared at him. "But I'm not totally sure . . ."

"It's enough," he said gravely, "for now."

He moved from the doorway. Chin up, and quickly in case he changed his mind, she swept past him, just as an anxious voice echoed hollowly up the stairs, "Ros? Are you up there?"

"I'm coming, Jason," she called back.

"We've been looking all over for you, girl," her father grumbled as she flew down the stairs two at a time.

"Well, I'm here now," she said brightly, "and I do think we ought to be going." She took her father's arm urgently. "It's much too damp and cold for you in here." She breathed a silent prayer that Paul Burford would keep out of the way for just a few more minutes. "Come along . . ."

But too late. Bill was peering past her at the other figure already on the stairs.

"Who's this then?" he asked suspiciously. "Snoopers?"

He was a soft-footed grey ghost in the shadows, even the beacon of his red hair muted by the gloom. And, as if he were a real ghost, bringing with him the invisible threat of unknown forces at work, Ros felt her breath catch in her throat with alarm and goose bumps prickle her skin as he brushed past her.

"Mr. Jago?" he said pleasantly. "I've been wanting to meet you. I'm Paul Burford."

Then, as her father stared with grimly deepening comprehension at the red-headed man, she also had the dismaying presentiment that the events of today were like catspaws of wind rippling the surface of a calm sea—bringing the threat of stormy waters ahead.

3

SLEEP eluded Ros that night. Every time she closed her eyes the scene leapt into her mind with horrid clarity. Paul Burford standing there relaxed and smiling, his hand outstretched. And her father slowly and deliberately turning his back then stalking away, outrage and scorn almost audible in the echoing beat of his footsteps.

Ros went after him, hearing Jason rushing politely to fill the fraught little silence with some technical point about foundations. Yet her last glimpse of Paul Burford as she fled was of his wry, enigmatic smile and the glint of amusement in his grey eyes as he lifted a hand in farewell.

Somehow his tolerant reaction heightened her embarrassment and discomfiture. If he had snarled and sworn she would have leapt to her father's defence without a second thought. As it was she felt oddly disconcerted—disorientated almost; as though opposing forces had clashed head on and she was caught in the middle, unsure of which way to turn.

Bill had gone straight to bed when he got back from the yard and at breakfast he remained gruff and uncommunicative behind the morning paper. Ros, gritty-eyed and yawning, consigned Paul Burford, his minions and his plans for the boatyard to the muddy depths of the creek, then resolved to put the whole thing out of her head. It was too perfect a morning to waste a second of it in brooding on a situation that couldn't be altered. And if she could get Dad out of the house for a few hours it would surely help to give him a new perspective.

"We'll go for a picnic," she announced.

The newspaper rustled a denial.

"You can choose where," she went on firmly.

"I don't feel . . ." he began.

"You can think about it," she interrupted briskly, "while I go down to the shop for bread."

He muttered grumpily behind the paper but at least he didn't turn the idea down flat. Ros grabbed a basket before he could dream up some excuse and went out into the sunshine, breathing deeply of the fresh scents rising from sun-warmed foliage as she strolled down the twisting lane that led to Fore Street.

She didn't hurry. For the first time since she'd returned to Pengara she found herself assessing her surroundings in the instinctive, searching way that had almost deserted her in the last traumatic weeks. There was that arresting glimpse of the creek between the houses, an interesting roof line of sagging slates and crooked chimneys, the ragged shape of a wall over-grown with massive valerian clumps . . . She felt a sharp, inward snap of exhileration, her fingers itching for a pencil or paint brush to capture and hold the essence of what she was seeing. She'd begun to believe she'd lost her enthusiasm —but now it was tumbling back, filling her mind with images and colour . . . and with a reawakened sense of purpose.

She walked cheerfully into the village shop—and almost marched straight out again. Dolores Partington, in black suede trousers and voluminous purple shirt, was holding a mainly one-sided conversation with the proprietor, Mrs. Jackson who, though the shop had long since been converted to self-service, had left her till to scuttle about fetching packets and jars to add to the Everest of goods on the counter.

"That will be all," Dolores announced in ringing tones. "You will deliver to the house by midday, if you please."

"Oh, but I'm not sure . . ."

"By midday!" Dolores' dark eyes flashed. The heavy gold bracelets on her arm clattered as she gestured imperiously, almost dislodging a display of biscuits. "Later is not convenient. These are necessities for my household. Or should you prefer that I take my custom to Truro?"

"Oh, no," Mrs. Jackson stammered.

"By midday, yes?"

Mrs. Jackson nodded meekly. Dolores, satisfied, swept a last regal glance round the shop. Ros tried to make herself invisible behind a pyramid of baked bean tins.

But Dolores, with a cry of recognition, was already bearing down on her.

"It is our kind friend of yesterday," she boomed, to the interest of several aged ladies waiting at the post office counter. "To you I owe my greatest thanks for your invaluable attentions to my dear friend Paul. He has told me everything: how you were a veritable—how do you say? Samaritan?"

"Hardly that," Ros protested.

"But you were kind!" Dolores cried. "And I was not kind at all." She pressed her hands to her majestic bosom in an apparent agony of remorse. "Say that you forgive me!"

"There's absolutely nothing to forgive," Ros said, acutely embarrassed. "Don't give it another thought, please."

Dolores beamed. "So modest." She leaned forward arms outstretched. Ros, fearing she was to be taken into an embrace, stepped hastily once more into the precarious shelter of the baked beans but Dolores was merely intent on riffling among the boxes of chocolates ranged on a shelf.

"Please accept this with my profoundest apologies," she said graciously pressing the largest, gaudiest box into Ros' hands. "I am sure Paul would wish you to have some small token of his gratitude."

Then, pausing only to command Mrs. Jackson to charge it to her account, she swept out of the shop, leaving Ros feeling that she should perhaps bob a curtsy or tug a humble forelock at Dolores' retreating back.

A buzz of whispers broke out among the pensioners. Mrs. Jackson was obviously dying to know what services Ros had rendered to Paul Burford to merit recognition by that snooty foreign woman who usually treated the villagers as a lower form of life. Ros, smiling too brightly, escaped from the shop with her groceries, suddenly feeling young and vulnerable under Mrs. Jackson's curious and censorious gaze, knowing that as soon as she was out of earshot the interesting titbit of gossip she and Dolores had provided would be well chewed over.

Walking back to the cottage she relaxed and grinned. For a minute there she might never have been away from Pengara. That one incident had pinpointed the claustrophobia of village life that had stirred her teenage self to rebellion.

"It's like living in a goldfish bowl!"

she'd stormed to Gwen. "I can't wait to get away."

Her sister had shrugged. "I can't see myself living anywhere else."

"But don't you feel stifled? I mean, you can't even sneeze without someone reporting back to Dad that you've caught cold because you were seen having a swim —naughty, naughty—when you should have been indoors doing your homework."

"Better that than living in some impersonal city where nobody gives two hoots if you're at death's door with pneumonia," Gwen said mildly. "I'd hate that."

"But you don't really know what it would be like. How can you without giving it a try?" The fifteen-year-old Ros had flung her arms wide. "There's a whole world out there waiting for us. I can't wait to explore it, to live life to the full. Oh, it'll be so exciting!"

Ten years on she could chuckle at her starry-eyed teenage dreams of the fame and fortune that awaited her once she left Pengara. It had been a whole lot tougher and a good deal less romantic than she'd expected. But hard work, tenacity and sheer determination had kept her going through the early confused months of adjustment and loneliness, and to the unexpected bouts of homesickness that had devastated her. She'd come through, though. Made good friends, steadily carved out a fulfilling career and a satisfying lifestyle for herself.

It was an ironic twist of fate that home-loving Gwen had fallen head-over-heels for an American searching out his Cornish roots and was now living blissfully in New York's concrete canyons, while she, Ros, had to adjust once more—however temporarily—to the limitations of living in a village.

Auntie Vi, trowel in hand, called "Good morning" from her garden gate at the corner of the lane and beckoned Ros over, looking worried.

"I've been watching out for you, m'dear, while I've been weeding my rose beds," she said. "I heard that Mr. Langley's been causin' a bit of bother this morning."

"Not again," Ros groaned.

"Not allowing nobody to go near the yard now the workmen are moving in. Told 'ol John Pritchard no one's to use the slip any more and any dinghies left there's to be moved off."

"But it's the only place you can launch at low water!"

"Him and John had a right set to about it, I believe. Don't make no odds, though. 'Orders from above,' he says." Auntie Vi's chins wobbled mournfully as she shook her head. "These newcomers. Don't take no note of what's customary. 'As to come in and start making changes."

"That's one change I won't let him make," Ros said grimly.

"Don't see as how you can stop him. That Langley's made it clear."

"Not Langley. His boss."

That man! She tried to concentrate as Auntie Vi launched into a rambling anecdote about the time when someone from up country had wanted to move the war memorial in order to extend the holiday house he'd just bought, but the memory of Paul Burford's enigmatic smile distracted her. All that smooth talk about bringing new life to the village was a lot of baloney. He didn't really care about the people of Pengara—only about getting his own way and making more money to add to his inherited loot.

"I'll sort it out," she assured Auntie Vi. "He won't trample down Pengara with his outsize hobnails," she added to herself stalking into the cottage. "Not if I can help it."

She didn't argue with Dad when, with an air of triumph, he announced that a picnic was out of the question today. "Doctor said he might call in this morning. Don't you remember?" he said craftily.

"No," she said, giving him a severe look. "But as it happens I have some business to attend to. Won't be long. Tell you about it later."

Bill looked almost comically taken aback at his easy victory, but Ros was too busy organising her arguments to take any notice.

By the time she reached Kelrozen she had her guns primed to fire a few telling salvos. Paul Burford wouldn't know what had hit him, she thought with grim satisfaction. But the sight of the big house, serene and austerely beautiful in the sunlight, slowed her indignant footsteps.

She hadn't had a really close look at it since it had been rescued from the sleazy state into which it had fallen in recent years. She could remember the time— before its fortunes had ebbed into a succession of mediocre ventures as a guest house, then holiday flats—when it had been a family home. But it had never looked so well as it did now. Its pristine paintwork and sparkling windows, its newly gravelled drive flanked with trimmed hydrangea bushes that would soon be a mass of blue blossom, spoke of loving restoration—and a great deal of money extravagently spent.

The front door stood temptingly open. She couldn't resist. Before she rang the bell she peered into the large square hall with its curved staircase sweeping away to the upper floor. She saw, with approval, the satiny gleam of the original floor-boards, an old brass-bound sea chest set against one white wall, a large blue and white Spode vase with an arrangement of golden foliage against another . . . an overall impression of light and space and elegance . . .

"Like it?"

Paul Burford had moved with predatory silence from an inner room.

"There was no one around. I was just going to ring . . ." she said, cheeks flaming and greatly put out to have been caught gawping.

"Come right in," he said easily. "We were just going to have coffee. Do join us."

She glared at him. "I'm not here on a social visit."

"Pity." He raised his eyebrows. "Do I get the feeling you're about to play hell with me about something?"

"The latest bit of nastiness down at the yard, actually," she said, adding with a note of triumph, "And don't think you can talk your way out of this one. Langley says you've issued the orders—the slip out of bounds and all dinghies to be removed."

"Ah, yes. Very upsetting." He looked anything but upset. "From time immemorial," he said in mock Mummesetshire tones, "the people of Pengara 'as launched their coracles from Jago's slip . . ."

"That's right, take the Mickey," she cut in furiously.

". . . but 'tis true," he went on blithely

as though she hadn't spoken, "that where one slip closes another opens."

"You don't give a damn! Never even bothered to discuss it with anybody . . ." She broke off, then asked cautiously, "What did you just say?"

He grinned and walked over to her and in an insufferably calm way patted her arm.

"There, there," he said comfortingly. "No need to get all worked up. It's all taken care of."

She snatched her arm away. "What do you mean?"

"Think about it. Where's the only other slip? Not as convenient I grant you . . ."

"The one here? At Kelrozen? But . . ."

Patiently, as though humouring a fractious child, he said, "The yard's going to be swarming with workmen and heavy machinery for quite a while. I couldn't possibly risk anyone having an accident. So I have suggested Kelrozen's slip as a temporary alternative. I've had the path unblocked," he added, forestalling her next question.

"But Langley said nothing of all this!"

she protested, clinging to the last shreds of righteous anger.

"Really?" For the first time the laughter in his grey eyes died. "That settles it. Our Mr. Langley's days in Pengara are numbered," he said with silky menace. "I've made a few interesting phone calls this morning. You were quite right. His motives don't bear too close a scrutiny. And there've been one or two other murky incidents in the past that are being looked at right this minute." If there was mockery in his eyes now, it wasn't aimed at her but at himself. "And I've you to thank for putting me straight."

The carpet had been well and truly yanked from under her feet and she felt at a distinct disadvantage under his understanding gaze. An uncompromisingly open and honest gaze she had, at last, to admit to herself. "Well . . . thank you for your explanation," she said stiffly. "I'll make sure everyone is informed about the new arrangements."

"Talking of new arrangements," he interrupted, "you still haven't told me what you think." He gestured at the hall with one large hand. "About all this."

"You seem to have done a good job," she said, then, because that sounded bit grudging, she added, "I'm glad the old place has found a caring owner."

"And I do care," he said gravely. "Not only about Kelrozen but about the village and the people in it."

She felt the gentle reproof in his voice and flushed.

"You must admit I had grounds for not quite believing that," she said quietly.

He nodded. "That creep Langley has a lot to answer for. He's going to be damned sorry for thinking he could get away with crooked dealing on my territory." Again that steely menace hardened his voice. Ros was glad she wouldn't be in Langley's shoes when the showdown came. "So what now?" he went on. "Do you and your father go on viewing me as public enemy number one? Or do we start again with the slate wiped clean?"

She hesitated. She wanted to cling to her old certainties that Paul Burford was a shady character without principles. But she honestly couldn't.

"I can't answer for my father," she said crisply. "For myself—well, I confess that Langley's activities have coloured my view of you." She held out her hand. "I'm willing to back my own judgment from now on."

He took her hand and held it. His palm was rough and warm against hers. There were callouses there—it wasn't the soft, cared-for hand of a desk-bound city gent. Despite his slicked down hair, immaculate cream sports shirt and faultlessly creased olive-brown slacks, she had a sudden vision of the crumpled, amiable hiker she'd first seen.

The thought made her smile more warmly than perhaps she'd intended.

He looked at her in silence for a long moment, then he said softly, "I'm glad we can be friends, Rosenwyn."

"My friends call me Ros," she said.

"Pity. Rosenwyn's a pretty name. Is it Cornish?"

"It is. It's a family name, too." She glanced at him mischievously. "Did you realise that your house is named for a several-times great-grandmother of mine?"

"Kelrozen?"

63

"It means Rose's Bower—or something like that." She glanced over to where the sea chest stood. "The first Rosenwyn Jago's portrait used to hang on that wall. I remember when my mother used to bring us to see Great Uncle Pedrek she would stand us in front of it and tell us the whole romantic story."

"Ah, I always guessed Kelrozen had a romantic history," he said with satisfaction. "Now, I insist you come in for coffee and fill me in with all the details."

"I ought to be going," she said doubtfully. "I said I wouldn't be long . . ." But suddenly there didn't seem any reason not to stay for a few minutes. "Well, I could sink a coffee," she admitted.

"We're in the garden," he said, leading her quickly—as though she might change her mind—through double doors to what she remembered as a sombre brown drawing-room full of dark furniture. Now it was all pale, sunny colours and comfortable squashy chairs. A door at the far end led to the Victorian conservatory. He took her through its leafy, jasmine-scented confines and out on to a new stone-flagged patio where loungers and white tables stood shaded by big lemon and white striped umbrellas.

Tania Partington lay on one of the loungers. She smiled in a friendly way and, as Paul made the formal introductions and busied himself pouring coffee into stoneware mugs, Ros wondered, not for the first time, how the dark, dramatic Dolores had managed to produce such an ethereally delicate-looking daughter. The white broderie anglaise sundress, the wispy fair hair lying loosely over creamy shoulders, the pansy-brown eyes staring ingenuously out at the world, seemed to emphasise her fragility and youth. Yet, Ros realised with surprise, she was older than a passing glance revealed—probably nearer twenty than the sixteen Ros had supposed.

"Right, fire away," Paul said, stretching his long length on to the lounger next to hers, the stoneware mug almost lost in his big hands.

She felt curiously hesitant. It was one thing to dream over the story that had always charmed and touched her in an indefinable way. Perhaps because her mother had named her for that far-off ancestor—as she had, equally romantically, named her other daughter Guinevere after the lady whose name was woven into the Arthurian legend. It was quite another to tell it baldly to people who were, after all, practically strangers.

"Oh, it's probably grown in the telling down the years," she began with a dismissive gesture. "The house was built by one William Jago for his bride, Rosenwyn. He was a sea captain, the war with Napoleon was at its height—and he just didn't return from a voyage to Portugal. News filtered through that the ship's cargo had been pirated by the French and the ship sunk with all hands."

Despite her diffidence her voice unconsciously warmed, her eyes seemed to take on extra sparkle, as she related how Rosenwyn Jago, left with four young children to feed and clothe had clung tenaciously to her belief that her husband was not dead. Practically penniless, their fortunes having foundered with their ship, she had determined to keep the house ready for William's return. She had started a school, set up a modest cottage lace-making industry, grown vegetables in her gardens, kept pigs in the stables and a cow on the front lawn. She had resisted the advances of a rich Truro landowner who had fallen in love with her. There was only one man for her: William. And after two long years her faithfulness was rewarded. William, haggard, thin and ill, with a horror story of being washed ashore, wounded and half drowned, being nursed by French peasants, captured when trying to stow away on board a fishing vessel and incarcerated in a noisome French prison where he had survived typhus and near-starvation until his release after Napoleon's final defeat, at last limped up the drive and into the arms of his faithful Rosenwyn.

"And he insisted," Ros said, "that every night, he had seen his wife's face in his dreams and heard her calling him back to Kelrozen. It was that, he said, that had kept him alive—in his words—'when death and despair had me in its inexorable grip'." She paused, her face dreamy. "That was when he had the portrait painted."

"So that she would remain forever as he had seen her in his dreams?"

"Something like that," she said, glancing at him from under the heavy fringe of her dark lashes. But he wasn't teasing, merely watching her with a small, warm smile hovering at the corners of his mouth.

"And what happened to the portait?"

She frowned. "I think it was sold with the house after Uncle Pedrek died. It was a huge great thing. My mother would have liked it, I know, but would hardly have got through the door of our cottage."

"It certainly wasn't here when I looked the place over," Paul said. "Mind, there's still a lot of stuff lying around the cellar I haven't got round to sorting through."

"Probably thrown out," Ros said with a pang. "The painting wasn't valuable."

"Except to the family," Paul said softly. "To you."

She shrugged, glanced away from his intense gaze, and was saved from answering by Tania saying with a sigh, "Such a lovely story. And with a happy ending. Oh, how I wish . . ." she broke off on what sounded suspiciously like a sob. Her brown eyes were swimming with tears.

Ros felt stricken. What had she said? Paul shook his head as though to absolve her of all blame, then reached over and took Tania's hand, cradling it between his own with the utmost gentleness.

"Oh, I'm sorry," Tania said, wiping the back of her free hand across her eyes in a childish gesture. "But the story . . . When the guerillas let us go and kept Daddy . . . Mother and I hoped and prayed . . . but it wasn't to be . . ."

"Tania and her parents were visiting Dolores' family estates in South America last year," Paul explained to a stunned Ros. "There was a coup. Their estates were confiscated, the family taken as hostages. Tania and Dolores were released, and escaped the country but her father— well, he was not so lucky."

"They shot him!" Tania burst out. "Stood him against a wall and shot him."

"How dreadful!" Ros gasped.

"Your story touched a painful chord," Tania quavered. "But you mustn't blame yourself. You weren't to know. And Paul here," she turned her limpid eyes to him with tremulous affection, "has been a tower of strength. Not least by giving us sanctuary in his lovely house until the lawyers have sorted out our financial affairs. I can't think what we would have done without him."

Ros was stunned to silence. She could think of nothing she could usefully say. Paul's few terse sentences, outlining the ugly events that had brought tragedy to Dolores and Tania, seemed to have cast a shadow over the bright sunshine. And though Tania was making painful efforts to suppress her anguish, Ros felt instinctively that her presence was only causing the girl to bottle up emotions that might be better released.

After a few moments she tactfully stood up.

"I really do have to be going," she said quietly, then to Paul who made to leave Tania's side, "No—please, I can see myself out."

Paul cast her an appreciative glance. Her last glimpse of them as she slipped away was of Tania's head close to Paul's, her hand clinging to his.

It was a picture that stayed with her in an odd haunting way as she made her way home.

4

A CAR pulled up beside her as she walked back through the village.

Jason Penrose leaned over and opened the passenger door.

"I've been down to the site," he said, "so I thought I'd call and see how your father was before I went back to the office. I was quite worried about him last evening. He seemed rather upset."

"No more than usual," she said with a sigh.

"Want a lift home?"

"Thanks," she said, sliding into the passenger seat with a feeling of relief. How solid and earnest and normal he looked in his dark grey business suit and discreet tie. The ugly and garish images Tania's story had conjured up seemed to have lodged sickeningly in her mind. She felt she needed something—somebody—to help clear her head.

"I had heard something about it," Jason said when she'd unburdened herself.

71

"Dolores and her English husband were friends of Paul's parents. When he heard they were back in England and having to sell their London house—most of their money having disappeared in the coup— he invited them down here. They were both in a pretty bad state, I believe. Tania was close to a complete breakdown, poor girl."

"No wonder it didn't take much to upset her today," Ros murmured.

"Dolores comes from a powerful and wealthy landowning family," he went on. "Now they're scattered—crushed by the new regime, their land confiscated."

Ros thought—with a sympathy and understanding she hadn't felt before—of Dolores sweeping about the village in her autocratic way. It wasn't a pose. She'd been born and bred to wealth and a knowledge of her own privileged position. It was to her credit that she could still hold her head high and show a bold face to the world after all she'd been through.

"Come in and have a bite of lunch with us," Ros said when Jason pulled the car up at the garden gate. "I was thinking of taking Dad out for a picnic, but he's probably thought up yet another excuse."

"If you're sure it wouldn't be too much trouble?"

"I'd be glad of the company," she said frankly. "But you know how things are—it means lashings of gloom and doom from Dad to accompany your homemade pâté and salad. If you'd rather not, I'll quite understand."

"I'll take a chance," he said with a smile.

Ros could have hugged him. Indeed, she did an hour later when she waved him off. He'd helped to make lunch outdoors in the tiny walled back garden a jollier meal than in many a long day.

She briefly told her father about Paul Burford putting the Kelrozen slip at the village's disposal and before he even had time to compose his face into a glower, Jason had sidetracked him with a question about a shrub growing against one wall. Then, when they'd settled to their meal he and Ros reminisced about their school days. He had the happy knack of listening attentively to her father's occasional dour comments, then gently and tactfully leading the conversation back to more cheerful topics. And when he got up to go and said, "That was great, Ros. We must get together again. How about dinner one evening?" it was her father who'd put in quickly, "Course you must, girl. Be a change for you. I'll manage for once."

"Congratulations," she said as they went out to the car. "You've just been awarded the William Jago Seal of Approval."

Jason smiled. "Diplomacy's my middle name. But you do look as though a night on the tiles wouldn't do you any harm, Ros."

"Heavens!" she laughed. "Do I look that bad?"

"Just a little peaky," he said earnestly, then went on, "I've sussed out a good wine bar since I've been back. Not terribly grand but they do super sea food." He glanced at her almost anxiously. Under the self-confident adult veneer she seemed to catch a glimpse of the studious, shy schoolboy she'd always felt just a little sorry for as he'd hovered uncertainly on the fringes of the crowd.

"That'll suit me fine," she assured him gently.

He looked relieved. "Pick you up at eight on Friday? Good. See you."

"A nice, steady sort of young chap," was her father's verdict before he settled to doze away the afternoon in his armchair, stubbornly refusing Ros' entreaties for him to enjoy the fresh air in the garden. "Sun's too bright. Makes my head ache," he said, closing his eyes and the conversation.

Ros stifled a sigh and went to wage war on the overgrown borders that had once been her father's pride and joy. She wished she could think of something to reawaken his interest in the garden—in anything. But he'd rejected every suggestion. "It'll take time and patience," the doctor had warned. "His heart attack gave him a nasty scare. And though he's making excellent progress physically, he's still frightened and insecure. Pity about losing the boatyard, though. That might have given him just the incentive he needed to get back to his feet."

Everything, inevitably, came back to that.

She'd been putting off removing the dinghy from the slip all day. The sun had set by the time she pulled on a sweater and went down to the yard.

House martins swooped and twittered above her head. Each year they returned to rebuild their nests under the eaves of the workshop and boat sheds. She wondered sadly where they would go this year. Already the yard seemed an alien place. Scaffolding had sprung up round the workshop, old slates torn from parts of the roof were stacked in piles on the ground, a big yellow digger stood like a sleeping monster by the trench it was gouging out of the black earth. And everywhere there were notices warning against trespass.

She was a trespasser now.

The knowledge jarred along her nerve ends. She felt a bleak echo of her father's bitterness surge through her. Abruptly she turned away and walked quickly down to where the dinghy lay by the slip. She'd struggled hard to be objective. She didn't want to be infected by Dad's corrosive resentment. But now, at this moment, with the harsh evidence of change all about her, it was difficult not to remember that if the red-headed man hadn't come along with his money and his urge to possess the yard, everything might have been very different. Dad might have plodded on in his own slow and uneconomic fashion for years. He might even have kept his health and his contented way of life.

She jammed the oars fiercely into the rowlocks and pulled away from the slip. A lemony-green afterglow lingered in the western sky, though the colour had soaked away from the land, leaving the wooded banks broodingly dark. Birdsong echoed across the creek. Soon that last vibrant chorus would die away and a magical tranquil stillness would envelop the land, the water, the village.

She stopped rowing and rested on her oars. This was what she had missed most when she was homesick and tired and overwhelmed in the racketty city. She had always kept in a corner of her mind the memory of a summer evening such as this to bring her comfort. Now, as the gentle current nudged the dinghy along, she let the peace soak into her troubled thoughts and weave its mysterious soothing spell.

She was quite restored to calm by the time she had tied the painter to the line of new posts that had been conveniently sited by Kelrozen's sea wall. She'd passed on the news of the new arrangement, as she'd promised, and several dinghies and tenders were already neatly stowed along the fore-shore. The rest would doubtless follow in the next few days. She'd spent a good half an hour on the phone smoothing down ruffled feathers, explaining about Langley, putting in a good word for Paul Burford —done quite a good PR job for him, in fact. She could sit back now in the sure knowledge that he'd gone up a notch or two in the village's cautious estimation.

For herself—well, for all her good intentions, it wasn't so easy. She wanted to be fair to him, but it was as though some inner early warning system that had been alerted at that first meeting, con-tinued to sound alarm bells.

She moved quietly along the track that skirted Kelrozen's lawns. It was true. He'd had the barrier that had blocked the way to the village removed. Instead, she saw with a jolt, he stood there himself, a bulky figure in the dusk, lounging against a fence post.

She stopped dead.

"I saw you on the creek," he said. "I was waiting for you."

"For me? Why?" She managed to keep her voice steady.

"I wanted to thank you," he said easily.

"For what?"

"For what you did for Tania today."

"Me? But I . . . I upset her."

"Precisely." His smile was warm. "Do you know she's never cried once since her father was killed? That's been half her trouble—she couldn't let go. She bottled everything up. Somehow what you said . . . it just unlocked the floodgates."

"Has she recovered now?"

He nodded. "She had a little nap and you could see as soon as she came downstairs that she was a whole lot better."

"If I'd only known . . ."

"If you'd known you'd have tiptoed round all sensitive topics—as we've been doing. And Tania would have still been hugging her grief to herself."

"Fools rush in . . ." she said lightly.

His grin flashed out. "Angels too, sometimes."

"I'm no angel," she said.

"How boring if you were."

The chorus of birds had fallen silent except for one noisy robin proclaiming his territory from a nearby oak. The growing darkness seemed to wrap them round in a warm, green-scented intimacy.

"I . . . I must go," she murmured.

She wished he'd move his unwelcome person from her path. He looked as though he was preparing for a long, cosy chat—and chatting with Paul Burford, cosily or otherwise, wasn't on her list of fun events. Then, treacherously, painfully, a tiny voice whispered another name in her head. If the man looking at her so intently had been Malcolm—here in the romantic twilight . . . She wrenched her thoughts away from that particular dead-end and made herself concentrate on what Paul was saying.

"I liked the way you told the story of the first Rosenwyn. You have a knack with words. I could almost believe it had happened just yesterday to people you know."

"I've lived with that story all my life. I know it by heart."

"And you told it with heart," he

said softly. "Is that the way you paint, too?"

She was getting a grip on her wayward emotions. She pondered the question seriously. "I suppose it is an essential ingredient for anything that's creative—be it painting a picture or . . . or making a beautiful garden. If you don't really care for anything but technique . . . well, it shows."

"My feelings exactly. Which brings me to my second reason for wanting to see you—that picture you were painting of the creek and the village. I'd like to buy it."

"It's only a sketch really. I was going to give it to Auntie Vi."

"Oh, yes. I remember you mentioned your aunt." He sounded disappointed. "Do you keep all your paintings in the family?"

"Auntie Vi isn't related. She's an unofficial aunt to everyone in the village. And to be honest the picture isn't the right colour for her. Doesn't match her new wallpaper."

He chuckled. "Ah, a true art connoisseur."

"Auntie Vi's a darling," Ros said spiritedly, "and at least she doesn't pretend. I'd rather paint a picture to go with Auntie Vi's curtains than for some poseur who thinks he knows it all and only buys something because it's trendy or will be a good investment."

"Will you sell me the picture if I tell you I don't know a great deal about paintings—but that one appealed to me instantly?"

"I . . . I'll think about it." Why did he keep on looking at her like that? As though, for all the gravity of his expression, laughter lurked a hairs-breadth away? It made her feel—well, she wasn't quite sure. Nervous? Awkward? And why was she arguing with him anyway? Anyone with half a grain of business sense would have been making an appointment to show him—a rich man with acres of walls to cover—a whole section of current work. Somehow common sense and Paul Burford made uneasy companions in her mind.

"Dad gets worried if I'm late," she said hurriedly, to cover the confusion of her thoughts. "May I pass, please?"

He stood to one side. "Don't let me keep you," he said, and as she squeezed past him on the narrow path he murmured, in a solemn whisper, "If it will help you to make up your mind, the picture will tone beautifully with the pattern on my bedroom carpet."

She made sure she was well out of sight before she allowed herself the luxury of a helpless grin.

She had too much to think about in the next few days to spare any thoughts for a man with red hair and wickedly teasing eyes. She was deluged with post that Susie had forwarded from London and she had to think seriously about future plans.

She desperately wanted to go back to London, to have the time and the space to get on with her work, but she knew she'd never rest happily knowing that Dad still needed her. If she left now there'd be no one to bully him into taking his exercise, keeping to his diet or trying to reawaken his interest in living. He'd just sink further down into his depression and self-imposed isolation.

The obvious answer was to get her gear down from London and work from Pengara for a while. But that posed a problem in itself.

She stared round the small, cramped bedroom that had been hers since she was a child. It was a pretty room and she loved it—but there was no way it would take her big drawing board, and the light filtering through the little dormer windows was totally inadequate.

She needed to set up some sort of a temporary studio where she could think and work without being disturbed—yet not too far from the cottage so that she'd be on hand for Dad.

The more she thought about it the more she liked the idea. Being away from Dad for some of the day might ease him back into independence; make him ready for the time when she had to make the final break to return to London for good.

She hammered away at her correspondence on Dad's old office typewriter and mentally reviewed and rejected every property in the village. Probably she'd have to go a bit further afield. Maybe Jason might know of somewhere.

She was looking forward to Friday evening. Pity her wardrobe was so limited. She'd come down to Pengara in a hurry when the weather had been chilly and wet. She hadn't been thinking about summery jaunts—more of keeping warm and comfortable while looking after Dad. She settled eventually on the one half-decent garment she had with her—a pale blue cotton jump suit. A wide white leather belt and some pretty white shell ear-rings she'd bought locally would dress it up a bit. It might not knock 'em for six in Truro but it was the best she could manage in the circumstances.

Auntie Vi, beaming, waved them off. Ros hadn't wanted to bother her but she'd insisted on keeping Dad company for at least some of the evening. "You'll go with an easier mind, m'dear," she'd said firmly. "I know how you'd worry."

"I don't know what I'd do without Auntie Vi," she confessed to Jason as he drove steadily along the narrow twisting lanes. "I really do hate leaving Dad alone —I feel if I turn my back he'll have a relapse or something."

He glanced at her sympathetically. "I know how you feel. When I was away at University my mother had to go into hospital for a major operation. I nearly flunked one of my exams, I'd spent so much time chasing up and down the country." He'd always been close to his widowed mother who'd now remarried and moved to North Devon. It was comforting to have someone to talk to who understood her worries. What's more, he was enthusiastic about her plan to set up a studio somewhere close to the village, promising to keep an eye open for a suitable place.

"Not a bad idea to spend the summer by the sea," he added.

"I'm just concerned with getting Dad through this bad patch," she said quietly. "And in a way, I feel a bit of a stranger here, now. I haven't spent a summer in Pengara since I was eighteen."

"But we could go swimming, sailing . . ."

"Hold on," she protested. "Apart from looking after Dad I've got work to do, remember? The kind that brings in the pennies."

"You need time off sometimes," he said sternly. "Like now. And as Auntie Vi, our village authority on these matters, has ordered you to relax that's just what you're going to do for the next few hours. OK?"

"OK, boss," she laughed. It was pleasant to be cossetted for once.

The wine bar, a rambling, low-ceilinged place with unexpected alcoves screened by clumps of greenery, was packed with people out to enjoy themselves, jollied along by a cheerful folk group twanging away in one corner. The whole ambience gave Ros' spirits a lift. They tucked into watercress soup followed by a seafood salad. Then, just as she was debating the merits of fresh strawberries and Cornish cream versus apple pie, the conversation struck a painful note. Such a casual question—he wasn't even looking at her, but gazing idly round the crowded tables.

"Nobody's tempted you into getting married then, Ros?"

Her hesitation drew his eyes back to her. She pretended a keen interest in the menu as she said lightly, "It was on the cards, but it didn't work out."

"I didn't mean to pry," he said quickly.

"I know." She pinned on a bright dismissive smile and, tactfully taking his cue, Jason called the waitress over to take the rest of their order.

"It didn't work out."

How easily the phrase had slipped off her tongue. How agonising the reality of coming to terms with Malcolm's almost casual rejection of the months of happiness they had shared.

"I've been seeing someone else, you see . . . I didn't mean it to happen . . . I hope we can be sensible about this, Ros, and part friends . . ."

Pride had stopped her from being anything but calm and grown-up about it. The storm had been inside, where she'd been devastated by the knowledge that while they were planning their future together, he was already, treacherously, seeing another woman.

The strawberries and cream arrived and they stuck to safer topics. But that casual question had rubbed some of the gloss off the evening, making her uncomfortably aware that it had become stuffily hot and the noise level seemed to have risen several decibels. She excused herself and went to the ladies' room where she swilled her cheeks with cold water and told herself severely that there were bound to be moment when she was reminded of

Malcolm's perfidy and she'd better get used to them.

Threading her way back through the tables she realised that Tania Partington was waving at her from one of the alcoves. She smiled and went over—and was at the table before she glimpsed, dismayingly, Tania's companion who'd been screened by a massive potted ivy. She might have guessed!

She murmured a polite greeting and prepared to move on smartly, but quick as she was, Paul was quicker. He was on his feet and had a firm grip on her arm before her brain had signalled "action" to her feet.

"Thought we might see you," he said smoothly. "Jason recommended this place. Said he was bringing you here, so we thought we'd give it a try, too. I'm glad we did. We've had a great meal." He gently pushed her into a chair. "You will join us for coffee and liqueurs won't you? And if you'll point me in the right direction I'll go and fetch Jason."

"The table round the corner," she said, "but I honestly don't . . ."

But he'd already gone. Tania smiled shyly at her. She looked extraordinarily pretty in a pale pink dress that on anyone else would have looked what it was—a shapeless swathe of designer wrinkles. On Tania it merely emphasised her delicate bones and her air of gentle other-worldliness.

"I do hope you don't mind staying to chat," Tania said softly. "It was my idea, really. When I saw you—I so much wanted to apologise for my—for the way I . . . I broke down when you were at the house the other day."

There was something appealing and forlorn about her tremulous smile.

Impulsively Ros touched her hand.

"I should be the one to apologise," she said. "I honestly had no idea what you'd been through."

The fair hair flew in fine wisps about her face as Tania shook her head vigorously.

"It was hateful. Vile. But I know I mustn't go on living in the past." She gripped Ros' hand. Her fingers were surprisingly strong despite their apparent delicacy. "Paul says I have to look to the future now. I think he's right." Again that wavering, shy smile. "I haven't got to know anyone in Pengara. Haven't wanted to, I suppose. But now I feel that has to change—and for a start I'd like to think that we could be friends, Ros."

"Sounds a good idea to me," Ros said, surprised and touched. There was something very likable about Tania. Pity, though, she mixed with such a doubtful class of person, she thought gloomily, her eyes drawn to the flaming beacon of Paul Burford's red hair as he shouldered his way back with Jason in tow.

Any idea that Jason might want to flee with her into the night were firmly squashed. He settled down contentedly with the air of a man who knows he's among friends and immediately dropped her right in it with an uncharacteristically tactless and crashing mistake.

"I've just had an idea," he said, with the excitement of a prospector who'd just seen the first glint of gold. "Ros is looking for somewhere to set up a studio for the summer. What about that hayloft you've been having done up above the stables at Kelrozen, Paul? Have you got any plans for it yet?"

Ros stifled the urge to kick him in the shins.

"No, I haven't. The builders have only just moved out," Paul said, thoughtfully. "A studio, eh?"

"Oh, I'm sure it wouldn't . . ." she began hastily.

"But I'm sure it would be," Paul cut in. "Suitable that is. Ideal, in fact." He raised his brandy glass as though to toast the suggestion. "Come up and see it tomorrow."

Jason and Tania beamed at her apparent good fortune. Ros managed a non-committal smile. Jason meant well, but she had already made up her mind. The less she had to do with Paul Burford the better. They might think him God's gift to Pengara, but she wasn't deceived. She distrusted that mocking, teasing light in his eye.

Her answer would be a definite no.

5

ROS walked up to Kelrozen the next morning cool and resolute. Whatever the charms of the room Paul was offering she would turn it down. The snag was, the moment she saw it she realised it was exactly what she wanted.

"Well? What do you say?" Paul stood with his arms folded across his scruffy T-shirt, uncaring that the clear morning light beaming through the uncurtained windows illuminated the gruesome condition of his shorts and the dollops of cement on his arms and legs. She averted her eyes from the unedifying sight and concentrated on the matter in hand. The room. And how not to be tempted by it.

But somehow she was disarmed—not least, if she was honest, by Paul himself. She'd found him rebuilding a partially collapsed old stone wall when, as he'd told her to last evening, she'd gone straight round to the stables.

She'd marched into the cobbled yard

words prepared, ready to be firm and stand none of his nonsense. She opened her mouth to call to him. Then clamped it shut, realising he hadn't seen her and it was her chance, for once, to study him unobserved.

She didn't question her motives. She just stood there, caught and held by the steady practised rhythm of his movements as he worked. There was nothing remotely polished about him now. Gone was the sleekly groomed look of last night—the smoothed down hair, the classy casual sweater and slacks. There was stubble on his chin, the red hair clung untidily to his forehead, a patch of sweat darkened the shoulders of his T-shirt. He looked like a man who'd got up early, grabbed the first old clothes that came to hand and gone out to get stuck into a job he enjoyed. He whistled softly as he worked, totally absorbed, until at last some instinct warned him that he wasn't alone. He glanced up and saw her.

Slowly he straightened his back. He didn't speak right away. He lifted his hand to shade his eyes from the sun. It was the sun, she reasoned afterwards, that played the trick—that made his expression so . . . so different, that caused her to respond to his smile with a warmth she certainly hadn't intended, but was stupidly unable to conceal.

Then it was over. The invisible link that seemed to bind them for a moment—the product, no doubt, of her all too vivid imagination—snapped. She forced her suddenly uncertain legs to move towards him.

"You're earlier than I expected," he said.

"You said any time this morning."

He grinned. "I always like to keep up certain standards when I'm alone. I'd hate you to get the impression I'm always as formally dressed as this."

The feisty spark was back in his eyes, she was relieved to see. Relieved? She wasn't so sure it was relief she felt. But at least on that level she knew how to respond.

"I'm completely outclassed," she admitted. "I hadn't realised that the slept-in look with tasteful cement trimmings was the in thing this year."

"We trendsetters like to be one step

ahead of the crowd," he assured her gravely.

"And building walls? That's a trendy thing to do, too?"

"That is pure indulgence. It's good sometimes to get back to basics." He spoke without pretension, not even jokily. He meant it. He held up his grubby hands. "Still, I'd better rinse this off before it hardens to cement gloves."

"You needn't stop on my account," she said briskly. "I do know my way around, remember? These stables were already in use as garages in Uncle Pedrek's day . . . and the ladder to the old hayloft was through here . . ."

She peered in through a half-open door, to where Dolores' stately black Mercedes sat—and was immediately flummoxed because the sagging, spidery beams and the ricketty ladder had been replaced with smooth walls and a new low ceiling.

"The entrance is at the end of the block, now," Paul said, pointing with a hand still dripping none-too-clean water from its rinse under the tap. "Come on, I'll show you the layout."

And now he stood waiting for her decision as she fought an inward battle between her heart which shreiked, "No", and her head which countered firmly with, "Yes, you ninny! You'll never find anything so perfect again."

It was one long white-walled room patched with sunlight from generous windows. A door at the far end led to a fitted galley-kitchen and a tiled bathroom.

"At the moment while Dolores is here to run the house we manage perfectly well with a couple of ladies coming up from the village to help out," he explained. "Eventually I'll have to get someone in to look after things when I have to be away. This will be the housekeeper's flat." He shrugged. "But that won't be for a while yet. Until then, you're welcome to use it."

And, boy, did she want to! She could put her drawing board there, where it got the best light . . . a table here to hold her brushes and pens and paints . . .

"You'll be completely private," Paul went on treacherously. "Here, catch." She grabbed the bunch of keys he threw at her. "You can lock the door and hang a DO NOT DISTURB notice on it. Dolores and

Tania won't bother you. I'll have to be away quite a bit—though I'm getting things organised my way—trimming the business down to the projects I'm interested in and so on to give me more time eventually in Pengara." The corners of his mouth twitched. "But when I am here I promise not to darken your doorstep." He lowered his voice seductively. "Unless, that is, you get lonely and decide to invite me up to see your etchings."

She turned her head to give him a chilling glance. But he was twirling imaginary moustachios and eyeing her with such a hammily theatrical leer that she had to take two or three paces up the room and pretend to be studying the view over the kitchen garden so that she wouldn't be tempted to smile.

"And the rent?" she asked crisply.

"To a friend, nothing."

She snapped round. "Then I couldn't possibly take it."

"You mean you're not my friend?" He slapped his forehead. "Why, last night I could have sworn you were beginning to think that you were. You actually laughed at one or two of my jokes. Remember?"

"Last night I'd drunk rather a lot of wine."

"Ah, *in vino veritas!*"

"Veritas, nothing, it merely clouded my judgment," she said with asperity, pushing down the memory of the surprisingly pleasant and lighthearted end to the evening when, at Jason's suggestion, they'd all driven down to a coast and had a midnight walk by the sea to blow away the stuffiness of the wine bar. "But if you really want the truth, here it is. Unless we come to a proper business arrangement I can't—won't—use this room."

"You don't want to be beholden to the big bad wolf? That it?" It was so close to her thoughts that she felt her cheeks grow hot. It didn't help that he looked insufferably complaisant, standing there, nodding sagely at his diagnosis. "And I thought we were putting all that behind us."

"I'm not looking for favours," she said between gritted teeth, "from you or anyone else." She made to throw the keys back at him. "So name your price. Or else . . ."

He held up his hands. "OK, OK, I submit."

He named a figure that was quite ridiculously small. She countered with one that hovered at her maximum limit. After a modicum of brisk bargaining they came to an agreement.

"I'll take it for a month with an option for another month," she said with a coolness that masked an entirely unbidden welling of excitement. Her fingers tightened over the bunch of keys. She couldn't wait to get her gear down from London, to have the time and the space to concentrate on the ideas that were buzzing in her head.

"You haven't forgotten about that picture I want, have you?" Paul reminded her as they went down the narrow stairs.

"It's yours," she said shortly. It seemed churlish to refuse him that now.

"And if you're working on any others while you're here, will you give me first refusal?"

"Sorry. I've got a backlog of commissioned work to catch up on."

They went out into the sunlit yard. She pulled the door close with a satisfying clunk. Her door, to her studio, however temporary. She already felt the same warm proprietory protectiveness towards it as she did to her studio at the London house.

"Then I'd like to add a few commissions to the list," Paul insisted.

"My publishers are pressing for the new book," she said without thinking. "I'm already behind with it."

"Which book's that?"

"Oh, just a book of fairy tales," she said lightly. After all, that had been Malcolm's description when, fired with the ideas that had taken hold of her, she'd shown him the first scribbled draft of the story, the roughs of the illustrations. He'd skimmed through them, smiled vaguely and said, "Very nice, love—but don't get too involved with it at the expense of your other work. I should think the market for fairy tales is pretty saturated." He'd kissed the tip of her nose. "I'd hate to see you build up your hopes only to be disappointed. Now, we'll be late for the film if we don't hurry."

Deflated, her confidence shaken, she han't spoken to anyone else about it. But something inside her just wouldn't let it go. She'd beavered away quietly in all her spare moments, the fantasy world that she'd invented becoming, through the months, almost as real as the gritty rooftops and chimneys she saw from her window. When it was finished she'd sent it off to a publisher with no great hopes. Now the author's copies—solid, glossy, beautifully produced—that Susie had forwarded on to her, lay in her bedroom. She still couldn't quite believe it, still felt inhibited about telling anyone. She hadn't even shown them to Dad yet. She'd grown used to seeing her illustrations in magazines and books, but this, somehow, was different; like putting a piece of herself on display for public criticism. Sometimes she wished she'd thought of using a pseudonym—then chuckled at herself for even believing anyone would be interested. Despite the publisher's enthusiasm over advance orders, the book would probably sink without trace.

But she could see questions about it—questions she indisputably didn't want to answer—hovering on Paul's lips. Luckily, he was diverted by Dolores who sailed into view looking as perfectly coiffured and rigged-out in her favourite scarlet as though several handmaidens had been at work on her since dawn. Ros was uncomfortably aware of her breeze-blown hair and old green cotton dress. Perhaps it was something to do with the way Dolores' expression froze when she saw Ros. It was not, Ros decided, a morning when boxes of chocolates and sweet thank-yous were to be pressed upon her.

"Paul, my darling," Dolores cried, "I have looked for you everywhere. Have you forgotten we were going out to choose new curtains for your study?"

"Oh, sorry, I had."

Dolores swept over to him and her voice rose several octaves as she saw the state he was in. "You must go and shower yourself. You have just the time to get changed." She smiled chillingly at Ros. "You will excuse us, will you not, Miss er . . . er . . ?"

"Ros is renting the stable flat for a few weeks," Paul explained. "I was showing her over."

"Indeed." At this piece of information Dolores' expression seemed to indicate several degrees of frost were forming.

"For a studio," Paul went on. "We were talking about it last night."

Dolores looked no happier. Or warmer. At a risk to her immaculately manicured hand she laid it on Paul's arm in a possessive way. "You are too easygoing, darling boy," she cooed, though Ros could almost hear the ice cracking on her lips. "You should not allow yourself to be distracted by these . . . these small matters when Tania and I are waiting for you. And you are to take Tania to lunch, remember." Dolores laid heavy emphasis on her daughter's name. "Then you dear young people are to visit some extremely pretty gardens, are you not, this afternoon?"

Ros could almost hear the "Keep Off" notices being hammered into the ground. If only Dolores knew! Tania could have him and welcome.

Paul, she saw with growing amusement, seemed for once to be at a loss for words. He looked for a moment like a man who was suddenly out of his depth and likely to drown.

She grinned broadly.

"Don't let me keep you," she said. "I'd

hate you to be late for all these important engagements." Then she added softly in a fair imitation of Dolores' accent. "You run along, darlink boy, and enjoy yourself."

But he caught it. She saw his scowl before she turned away, laughing. It quite made her morning.

When she got back to the cottage she went straight up to her bedroom and picked up a copy of her book. Then she braced herself and went down to join her father. Luckily Gwen's weekly letter had arrived with the morning's post. It was the one event of the week guaranteed to put Dad in an agreeable frame of mind, and she took advantage of it.

She sat down opposite him and explained what she planned to do, watching his expression lighten when he realised she wasn't going to go back to London yet, seeing the pride in his eyes as his fingers stroked the glossy cover of the book.

"When you told me about it," he said softly, "I didn't think it'd be anything as grand as this. A little children's tale, I thought it was." He opened it, read the loving message she'd written inside for him over her signature and cleared his throat for rather a long time before he said, gruffly, "Can't say that this sort of thing's my cup of tea, but it has handsome pictures and I promise I'll read every word if it takes me till Christmas."

She chuckled. "I hope it isn't that bad —but I know what you mean. You'd rather I'd written a good thriller." Though it was a long time, she thought sadly, since he'd even opened a book.

"And you're going to do another one like this?"

"That's what the publisher wants," she said. "Same characters—different adventures. I've done some roughs and scribbled a few ideas—but now I really have to get down to some solid work."

"Of course you must!"

"I've found the perfect studio. At least," she added, throwing in one name Dad wouldn't argue with, "it was Jason's brainwave."

Bill nodded approvingly. "Sensible young man, Jason," he agreed.

Now came the crunch. In a few short phrases she told him then sat back waiting for the storm. It didn't come but she could see he was hanging on to his temper with the greatest difficulty. Perhaps it was the solid proof of her achievement that swayed him, or the fact that she wasn't going to desert him and return to London. Whatever it was, he merely said grudgingly, "Well, you know my views, but if it's the only place . . ."

"It is, Dad," she said gently.

"It's important to you, this book, I can see that. And I wouldn't want to put obstacles in your way." He glared at her from under his shaggy eyebrows. "But just remember you're a Jago, that's all. And whenever you see that . . . that upstart, think of what he's done to us."

It was the one thing, she thought, as she went into the kitchen to prepare lunch, she was scarcely likely to forget.

She spent the next few days preparing for her trip to London. She rang Susie and made arrangements to stay overnight, prepared enough easy meals to store in the freezer to keep Dad going for a month, worried about going, until Auntie Vi said, "My dear soul, 'tis only a couple of days.

You'll be back before we've even realised you've gone."

She went up to Kelrozen a couple of times, secure in the knowledge that Paul had been seen leaving Pengara in his slinky red Porsche. On her second visit she was unloading a small table from her old hatchback when Tania drifted into view.

"I saw you drive up," she said. "Can I help?"

"You came just at the right time," Ros said cheerfully. "Could you give me a hand up the stairs with this?"

While Ros sorted out the contents of a plastic carrier bag, Tania wandered down the room. "I do envy you," she said eventually. "I mean, being able to draw and paint well enough to make a career of it." She shrugged her slight shoulders. "Me, I'm not clever at all."

"Perhaps you just haven't found anything yet that interests you."

"Oh, I've dabbled in lots of things," Tania sighed. "All the usual finishing school stuff—cookery, flower arranging and so on. I even did a secretarial course. The trouble is, I suppose, I've never really needed to earn my living." She smiled

108

impishly. "And though I take after my father in looks, I certainly didn't inherit his brains. He was very quiet and scholarly, content to spend his days in his library researching terribly boring stuff about dead languages. So different from my mother who's so . . . so outgoing. Yet they had a really happy marriage."

"The attraction of opposites," Ros said.

"That's it. They were very much in love." Her voice softened. "If I'm truthful, when I look into the future I can only see myself being one half of a partnership like that. That's all I want, really. Marriage . . . children . . . a home to run."

"And if I read the runes right," Ros thought, "your estimable mama has your future all neatly lined up for you."

Tania chatted on. Increasingly, Ros had the impression of a rather solitary, shy girl, dominated by her strong-willed mother, but in her quiet way searching for her own identity—even looking for a means to break out of Dolores' overprotective if loving guardianship; though perhaps that was something she didn't quite realise herself yet.

That she was fond of Paul and he of her was unquestionable. When she spoke of him—of how she was helping him with some of his paperwork and how he phoned each day while he was away—her voice took on animation and colour. Ros remembered how they'd teased each other and laughed that evening at the wine bar, comfortable and relaxed together. It was easy enough to imagine them living in Kelrozen, bringing up a brood of red-headed children . . .

Her thoughts shied suddenly from this picture as Tania delved into the pocket of her sun dress, exclaiming, "Heavens, I was nearly forgetting the object of my visit." She drew out a white envelope. "Here's your invitation."

"Invitation?" She opened the envelope and drew out the thick card. "A house warming party?"

"You must come," Tania insisted. "My mother's organising it for Paul—and she's a marvel, truly. Nobody misses her parties. Even last Christmas when we were both feeling so low, she insisted on carrying on as usual. All her friends came from London."

"So I heard," Ros said wryly, remembering the comments about it that had come to her ears.

"Then you'll accept?"

"I'll think about it," she said evasively, and stuffed the card out of sight in her bag.

"I've been invited too," Jason said that evening. They were sitting companionably in the garden, making the most of the last rays of the sun before it dipped behind the house. From indoors came the faint sound of canned laughter where Bill sat, as usual, hunched dourly in front of the television set. "Should be quite a party, I gather."

"Well, I won't be there to see it," she said.

"I was hoping we could go together."

She shook her head. "Count me out of this one."

He looked crestfallen, but he didn't press the point. They went on to talk of other things, but she felt that he was disappointed. He went a bit quiet and she caught him looking at her in an uncertain kind of way. It bothered her. She valued her friendship with Jason, but she wondered uneasily if he had begun to read something more than she intended into their relationship. He dropped his usual light kiss on her cheek as he left. But did his kiss linger a little? Did that arm thrown casually round her shoulders hold her for a fraction longer than was necessary?

She frowned as she went back into the cottage after waving him off. Why did life have to be so complicated? No way was she ready for another emotional entanglement. Malcolm had taken her love and thrown it aside as casually as if he were disposing of an old garment that had to be sent to a jumble sale to make room for a new one in the wardrobe. It would be a long time before the scars of that betrayal would heal—if they ever did. Sometimes she wondered if she would ever learn to trust again. In the meantime, she had no intention of stepping from the frying pan into the fire. She'd have to cool it with Jason. Which was sad because she appreciated his quiet good sense and kindness.

Some time in the night it began to rain. After the days of warmth and sunlight, she woke to a soft mizzle drifting across the window. The hills were blanketed with low cloud, the creek had turned to the colour of dirty pewter.

"Not a bad day to be leaving the land of piskies and pasties," she joked when she took her father his breakfast tray in bed and kissed him goodbye.

But she hadn't slept too well and as she went through the garden to the lane at the back where she kept her car, the heavy fragrance of wet earth and foliage rose seductively all around her. It was the sort of morning when she would have enjoyed pulling on wellies and going for a long tramp to clear her head of confused dreams of Malcolm that had left her feeling limp and vaguely out of sorts.

She switched on the car radio to a burst of pop music and firmly turned her thoughts to the drive ahead. She was returning to London, which was great, even if it was for only a couple of days. She was going to see her friends, catch up on the news, put her worries behind her for a little while.

But the increasingly heavy rain, the disc

jockey's inanities, the heavy traffic once she'd plugged into the motorway system across the Tamar, only made her feel increasingly irritable.

The journey was dreary and as she drove the last few familiar miles she got into a long, halting crawl of cars. Rain hammered down on the car roof and ran greasily along the littered gutters of the road. Grey buildings towered up to the lowering clouds. People scurried, head down, along the pavements.

But she loved the old place, didn't she? She loved its excitement, its noise—the sense of being a very tiny fish in an exceedingly large and turbulent pond.

Juddering along in the traffic jam she waited patiently for the uplift the thought of being back in London usually gave her. But it didn't. All that came into her head was a misty picture of the creek seen through veils of drifting rain—and she had to fight a sudden and disquieting urge to turn the car round and head west towards Cornwall.

6

ROS parked the car outside the tall house in a long grey street of respectable Edwardian villas. She lugged her overnight bag indoors and up two flights of stairs then went through her bedroom feeling uncomfortably like an intruder when she saw unfamiliar belongings scattered around. But the studio—which was actually half of the large top floor room partitioned off—was reassuringly the same. Apart from a camp bed that had been carefully made up for her, everything was as she'd left it.

She plunged straight in, making herself concentrate on dismantling her drawing board, packing everything she'd need in Cornwall neatly into boxes. She was used to working alone in the house, but today the emptiness seemed overwhelming.

She was glad to hear the sound of a key in the lock. Dee, who taught at a nearby school, was first home closely followed by Susie and the new girl, Angela. Lynn

115

breezed in last of all. It was a succession of hugs and greetings and exclamations of pleasure at the armfuls of budding roses, sweet william and still-damp greenery she'd brought with her and arranged in big vases in the living-room.

They'd prepared a special dinner.

"In your honour," Susie laughed. "So sit down, have a glass of something and watch us work our fingers to the bone."

And at last the genuine friendliness caught her up, shrivelling the last traces of the bleak mood that had been with her all day. She was even recovered enough, by the time they'd had dinner, to put the question she'd been dying to ask Susie.

"Seen anything of Malcolm?"

The others were tackling the washing up. Susie had brought in a tray of coffee. She handed a cup to Ros with a sardonic smile.

"The occasional unwelcome glimpse across a crowded room." Malcolm was on the administrative staff of the hospital where Susie was a pharmacist. "Still going with that girl from medical records— hasn't seen yet through the glamorous exterior to the lack of brain within."

"She's a very pretty girl," Ros said.

"More to the point, she has a doting daddy with his own chain of fast food outlets. Did you know that?"

Ros shook her head.

"If you ask me, I think our Malcolm's got his eye on Daddy's little empire as much as Avril's all-too-evident charms."

"But he isn't like that," Ros protested quickly.

"Isn't he?" Susie looked unconvinced. Then she said quietly, "Perhaps it's too soon for me to say this, love. I know you're still carrying a torch for the wretched man, but honestly, I think he did you a favour by transferring his affections to Avril."

"Oh, no . . ."

"Oh, yes," Susie went on in her forthright way. "I suspect that under the charm and good looks he has a heart of pure microchip silicone guaranteed to keep on making all the right calculations—for himself of course—for the rest of his life. I wouldn't envy Avril one little bit if I were you. You're better off without him."

Ros was shaken at her friend's judgment, but the others came in for their coffee then and she put it out of her mind as the evening proceeded on its lively way, ending with an hilarious hour spent trying on some of Lynn's cast-offs.

"Darlings, help yourselves. I haven't had a turn out for ages," Lynn cried, flinging armfuls of clothes on to the bed from her bulging wardrobe. "Anything you don't want goes straight to Oxfam. Susie, this blouse is just you—and Ros, I can see the Cornish talent lusting after you in this."

She thrust a goldeny silky something at Ros and though Ros had to agree that it was gorgeous, she couldn't imagine when she'd have the occasion to wear it.

Lynn insisted she take it. "That colour's marvellous with a tan, darling—and yours is coming along nicely. Fantastic material, too. Never creases, and you look terrific in it." She waved her fist threateningly. "If you don't take it with you, I swear I'll post it on to you!"

Ros laughed and later obediently stuffed it at the bottom of her suitcase, safe in the knowledge that she could leave it there when she'd unpacked the shirts, shorts and cotton dresses that she was transferring down to Pengara.

It was still raining when she left the next morning. It was only when she crossed the Devon border that the clouds lifted. On impulse she left the motorway at Exeter and took the route that would lead her across Dartmoor's breezy heights.

As the sky cleared to a deep, newly-washed blue and the sun dazzled from every puddle, she wound down the window and let the draught sweep through the car. She rejoiced at its fresh, cutting edge, in the vistas of heathery moorland, sweeping away to the horizon and, when she pulled over to the side of the road and switched off the engine, in the pure exultant song of the larks rising from the golden gorse.

She strolled a little way to stretch her legs, wishing her friends were with her to enjoy all this space and beauty. It had been lovely to see them, she thought wistfully, to pick up the threads again if only for a few hours.

A few yards away a pony cropped the grass, unconcerned at her presence. The tiny foal at her side suddenly erupted into leggy, awkward life, dashing across the grass, tossing its head, bouncing on its little hooves in the sheer physical excitement of being alive.

Ros' breath caught with delight at such a display of pure, joyous movement. She laughed aloud as, almost comically, the foal stopped its mad gambolling as suddenly as it had begun and ambled sedately to its mother.

Ros turned back to the car, the memory sharp in her mind of grey wet streets she'd driven through yesterday, the people huddling sombre-faced under their umbrellas, the traffic thundering blindly along. What a contrast to that burst of instinctive joy she had just witnessed. On these empty heights, that glossy, exciting picture she'd always had of London wavered and blurred. At this moment she wouldn't have swapped all the delights the city had to offer for the joyful display she'd just witnessed and longed to capture in paint.

She looked westwards across the tors sharply etched against the sky in the rain-washed air, feeling strangely content.

She'd be over the Tamar soon and into Cornwall. Home.

She was smiling when she got back into the car. Maybe Jason was right. A summer by the sea wasn't such a bad idea after all.

The following days took on a satisfying pattern. Once she'd got the studio to rights she plunged into work, revelling in the release of the images bubbling in her mind. As the pictures grew to glowing life under her fingers, so it seemed that one other facet of her life took on a more hopeful aspect. Her father had been so anxious for her return that, without any prompting on Auntie Vi's part, he'd walked down the lane and installed himself on the wooden bench by the War Memorial to watch for her car. She was so astonished at seeing him as she carefully negotiated that last awkward bend that she almost clipped the hedge as she stood on the brakes.

He'd climbed into the passenger seat, his only explanation a curt, "If you didn't see me with your own eyes, you wouldn't believe that I'd done as you'd said and had a bit of outdoor exercise."

"Oh, Dad, am I really such a cynic?" she laughed.

"You're a bossy boots, I know that. Don't give a man a bit of peace."

"It's for your own good."

"That's as maybe. Anyway," he added gruffly, "I'm glad you're back safely after your gallivanting."

She kissed his rough cheek.

"I'm glad, too," she said softly.

And now the new routine was established, he did really seem to be making an effort to please. Little things, true. The table carefully set for their meal, the garden path swept, an offhand offer to wash the dishes. But they were steps, however faltering, in the right direction. It gave her the first glimmer of hope for his eventual release from the chains of lethargy and depression that bound him; and for her own escape back to her life in London.

As the days passed and the new book began to take solid shape she knew she had much to thank Jason and Paul for: Jason for spotting the potential of the hayloft flat, Paul for letting her use it. But she was grateful that neither of them intruded into her privacy. Jason had phoned her one evening to apologise for not calling in person. "Hell of a rush on at the office at the moment. One of the partners is sick, another away on business."

"Don't worry," she said quickly. "We'll get together when we're both through this busy patch." And felt relief when she put down the phone that he hadn't pressed her to go out—or mentioned again the house-warming party.

But though she was so discreetly isolated from the house in her little eyrie above the garages it seemed that she was slowly drawn into the life of Kelrozen without actually being part of it.

She heard the comings and goings of cars: the rumble of Dolores' Mercedes, the throaty purr of Paul's Porsche. Standing to stretch her stiff limbs she would catch a glimpse of Tania crossing the yard with a handful of letters to take to the post or Dolores haranguing the gardener in the shrubbery or pacing round in deep conversation with strangers. Caterers, florists, overalled workmen came and went.

"Mother's in her element," Tania

explained when she met Ros on the studio doorstep one morning. "This party is occupying every spare minute. She's determined it's to be the best ever." She giggled. "She wanted to make it a theme party—ancient Rome with everyone dressed in togas, but Paul put his foot down. So now she's planning to bring the outdoors inside with an English country garden look and traditional Cornish food." She patted the business-like document case under her arm. "My contribution's running the errands. I'm just off to the caterers then I've some papers to drop in at Jason's office for Paul. Anything I can get you while I'm in Truro? No? Well, I go out most days, so if I can do anything for you, you will ask, won't you?" She looked quite serious about it. Dressed for the part, too, Ros thought with amusement, in a neat skirt and tailored blouse with her hair tied back into a plait, giving her the air of an eager schoolgirl playing at being grown-up.

"Paul asked me to look after you," Tania added earnestly.

Ros raised her eyebrows. "Did he now?"

"He told me I wasn't to bother you, but just make sure that you were comfortable and had everything you needed." She smiled shyly. "He thinks you're very talented."

"On the evidence of one picture?" she said, inclined to laugh.

"Oh, no! I think he's seen some of your other work. At least, he was saying something about it on the phone. He's in Birmingham this week. Back on Friday, though," she concluded, looking at Ros as though expecting her to share her own ingenuous pleasure at the thought.

Ros didn't. She marched upstairs and tried not to be distracted by thoughts of Paul making sure that she was being looked after. Of Paul—insufferable man—expressing the view that he thought her talented when he'd said himself he knew nothing about painting. It was a good half hour before the rhythm of her work caught her up completely.

On Friday she was washing her brushes before dashing home for lunch when she heard the Porsche purr into the yard. She hung back until she judged Paul had gone up to the house before she hurried down the stairs. But she opened the door to find him standing grinning on her doorstep, red hair tousled, tie pulled loose, one big hand holding a book. Her book. He held it up so that the cover with its striking jewel colours caught the light.

"Ah, you've just saved me from breaking my promise not to disturb you."

She managed a hesitant smile. "Is it something urgent? I was just going home for lunch."

"Urgent?" A severe frown replaced his grin. "I'll say. You're guilty of deception, Rosenwyn Jago. No, don't try to deny it. You tried to fool me. 'A book of fairy tales', you said. Trying to make me think you'd scribbled a twee bit of nonsense to amuse a few toddlers. This—" he wagged the book sternly under her nose—"is nothing of the sort."

"I didn't try to deceive you," she protested. "It is a fairy tale."

"A fantasy," he cut in. "An invented world, a clever mix of legend and magic and mystery. But for tinies? No way."

She shrugged uncomfortably. He refused to let her off the hook.

"As for the illustrations, well, no

wonder your publisher's screaming for the next one." He paused, his grin returning. "Have you read the reviews? Not so much glowing as incandescent!"

She thought uneasily of the local newspaper which had sent a reporter yesterday to interview her, of the way news of her success had gone round the village grapevine with the speed of light. Of the book signing session in Falmouth next week. She seemed to have set events in motion that threatened to be both a disturbance and a challenge. As the red-headed man's eyes challenged her now.

She said briskly, to disguise her inner uncertainty, "I'd be an idiot to get carried away by a couple of good reviews. This time next month it'll all be forgotten."

"Rubbish. You've got a best-seller on your hands," he said with conviction.

"That's just your opinion."

"And the opinion of the manager of the bookshop where I bought this. He says it's the sort of book that because it's so original and doesn't fall into any of the usual categories will either sink without trace or become a cult. He puts odds on the latter.

He says there's a terrific amount of interest and it's selling well already."

She was silent for a moment. Was it really a possibility that her book was going to be such a success?

"Don't let it scare you," he said softly, as though he caught the trend of her thoughts. "You should be proud of yourself. It's a terrific book."

"You've read it? I wouldn't have thought . . . well, that it was your sort of thing."

"Neither would I." His grey eyes were warm and compelling. "I confess that I bought it only because you'd written it. I meant to flick through it. Then found that I couldn't. Once I started to read I was hooked. I had to know what happened to those strange and comical little characters in their magical world. As for the illustrations—they're so detailed I'm still finding delights every time I open the book."

She swallowed. "It's very kind of you to be so complimentary."

"I'm not being complimentary," he almost shouted. "I'm telling you the truth. It's good. You're good. Believe it."

She laughed shakily. "Shush. If there were still horses in here you'd be frightening them."

"Who cares? I'll shout it to the whole world if you like."

"I don't like. I have quite enough trouble with the publishers setting reporters on me without you starting up as my PRO." She noted, inconsequentially, that laughter had left its tiny permanent marks round his eyes. And his lashes weren't red like his hair but a thick deep gold. "Now have you finished? May I go home for my lunch?"

"When you've signed my copy of 'Stormlands'." He put down his case, fished a pen out of his jacket pocket and held the book steady for her.

She hesitated. "What shall I write? I mean, I'm not used to this sort of thing."

"How about, 'To darling Paul who has made my next book possible'?"

She shot him a quelling look and settled for 'Best wishes' above her signature.

He closed the book and as she handed back the pen, his hand closed over hers. "Thanks," he said. And, before she realised his intention he raised her hand, turned it over and dropped the lightest of kisses on the inside of her wrist. All the time his eyes, wicked and teasing, watched her reaction; which was swift and angry. She snatched her hand back fiercely, as though his touch had burned.

"I'll say goodbye, then," he said with good humour that mocked her anger. "See you around."

She watched him lope across the yard with his long stride. So tall and relaxed and . . . and insufferably full of himself!

Then she jolted herself into action and, almost running, she made for home, rubbing her wrist as though trying to erase the memory of his touch.

She worked through Saturday resolutely ignoring the calm blue day outside the studio window. Her only distraction during the morning was the intrusive sound of happy voices from the yard below. Her hand paused in its careful interweaving of greenery around a tiny golden foal kicking its heels in the margin of one of her paintings, her gaze drawn inexorably to the window.

Dolores, Paul and Tania formed a sunlit

tableau below, Paul carrying a picnic hamper, his free arm slung casually round Tania's shoulders, Tania looking up at him, her brown eyes shining, her soft pink mouth curved in a happy smile. Paul glanced down at her with an expression that was both tender and affectionate and Dolores, Ros noted, watched them both with the smug air of a cream-fed cat.

When the Porsche had roared away and Dolores had marched off triumphantly about her own affairs, Ros returned grumpily to her drawing board. She'd grown used to the bustle of activities below her windows, but for some reason this particular interruption had thrown her. For the rest of the day she was aware of an odd restless feeling that couldn't quite be quelled.

Maybe she needed a break after so long working flat out. Perhaps that was why when Jason rang that evening her resolve to keep him at a distance crumbled under the prospect of a day away from Pengara.

"I've borrowed a sailing dinghy," he said. "Fancy a day out? Your father, too, of course. I've a quiet little cove in mind

131

where we can get the trailer down to the beach."

The cove was reached by lanes so narrow and twisting that few tourists bothered with it. There was plenty of space on the golden arc of sand to settle Bill in his deckchair where he could watch them with a critical eye as they rigged up the dinghy and launched it into the shallows. It was a long time since Ros had crewed a sailing dinghy, but she soon got back into the swing of it under Jason's calm instructions. It was exhilerating being out on such a perfect day, with the water slapping rhythmically under the dinghy's keel and her hands and mind fully occupied.

Later they picnicked handsomely on chicken and salad, they swam and sunbathed and the day slipped easily and pleasantly along. As the afternoon drew on and Bill settled for a nap, Jason and Ros scrambled up the thread of a path that zigzagged up the cliffs and strolled companionably along the rabbit-cropped turf.

She couldn't quite pinpoint the moment when the easy flow of their conversation dried up. But it did. And she wasn't sure if the silence that replaced it was really uncomfortable—or something she imagined because she was suddenly alert and on the defensive.

"Terrific view from up here," she said brightly, as they came to an outcrop of rock before the path dipped away down to the next cove.

Jason nodded, but though his eyes followed the direction of her finger as she pointed out distant landmarks, his thoughts, she could sense, were not on pretty views.

But what were they on? She had the feeling that they were on her. And that panicked her.

"Ros." He glanced at her, then away, shrugging. "Oh, never mind. We'd better turn back."

But that wasn't what he'd been going to say.

She didn't move, thinking of the pleasant day they'd spent together. The way they'd always been friends. She didn't want to spoil that, and how she reacted now was crucial to that friendship. Besides, she hated to see him looking as troubled as he did now. Better to clear the air and get the whole thing sorted out sensibly.

She took a deep breath. "Jason—is something bothering you?"

"You could say that."

"Want to talk about it?"

He looked undecided, then suddenly caught her hand. "Sit down a minute, Ros."

They sat with their back to the rock. He still held her hand. He stared beseechingly into her eyes.

"Here it comes," she thought with a pang of sadness. A pity. She valued Jason's friendship. Nothing would be the same again if he wanted their relationship on another footing entirely.

"I've been too busy until now to let myself get too involved," he said awkwardly, "that is, I've never met anyone I really felt I could spend the rest of my life with. Until now."

Oh, dear. She swallowed and frantically sought for soothing words. His eyes had a soft, pleading look. She was going to hate herself in the next few minutes when she had to give him the big thumbs down.

"I don't know what to do, Ros." And then he added with the air of a desperate man, "It's . . . it's Tania!"

"Tania!"

He shook his head in bewilderment. "I seem to have fallen for her. Head over heels. And try as I might I can't get her out of my mind."

7

THE weather broke the next day.

By three o'clock Ros had to switch on the light and as she stood by the studio window watching lightning throw the inky clouds into lurid relief, the Mercedes drove into the yard. Tania and Dolores hastily scrambled out, but the rain suddenly descended in a violent cascade and Ros flew down the stairs, flung open the door and called to them to come and take shelter in the studio.

Tania's face was colourless. "I can't help it—I loathe thunderstorms," she said as she perched tensely on one of Ros' two chairs.

Ros caught Dolores' eye sympathetically and set about distracting Tania from the tumult outside. She made coffee and chatted cheerfully before there was a terrific crack of thunder and the lights went off.

Tania squeaked with terror. Ros firmly pressed the coffee mug into her hands, and searched her mind for interesting subjects. Dolores, obviously with the same aim, asked to see some of Ros' paintings.

It was a command rather than a request, but Ros was happy enough to bring out some of her finished illustrations and saw that Dolores was pleased when Tania's attention was drawn away from the storm. Then the lights came back on, enabling them to study the wealth of detail in each glowing, jewel-coloured picture.

"You have much talent," Dolores conceded with the air of a queen bestowing an honour on a humble subject.

"They're beautiful paintings," Tania breathed. "When will you have the book ready?"

"It's coming along," she said. "The stories are all roughed out. Which reminds me, I have to contact a typist for the finished manuscript. I must see about that tomorrow."

"Oh, but couldn't I do it for you?" Tania looked at her eagerly.

"Well, I don't know," Ros said doubtfully. She didn't want to be unkind but she did want a professional job done.

"I'm a good typist," Tania declared

with unexpected confidence. "You can ask Paul—and I'm quite used to his word processor now. He wouldn't mind me using it for typing your book."

"My daughter has most excellent secretarial qualifications," Dolores said with maternal pride.

Ros, still hesitating, remembered what Jason had told her yesterday afternoon—how he found it impossible to get more than a few moments alone with Tania, how Dolores had such old-fashioned, Latin ideas. "If she could chaperone Tania everywhere, she would," he'd grumbled. "I think she sees all men as potential trouble. Unless the man is Paul Burford, of course. If you ask me she's only waiting for Paul to pop the question so that she can go ahead and plan the wedding of the year. And Tania's so gentle she'll be bull-dozed into marrying him without having a chance to discover that she does have a choice." He'd sighed heavily. "The trouble is Paul's pretty special to her—and of course he was let down badly by that New Zealand girl—"

"Oh?" Ros glanced at him sharply.

Jason shrugged. "He was due to be

married. The girl—Chrissie I think her name was—cancelled the wedding after he'd come over to England. Married someone else. He was pretty cut up about it I believe. Tania thinks it's all terribly sad and romantic, which gives him a distinct advantage." He smiled ruefully. "Yet for all that, I think she . . . well, I just feel if we could get to know each other properly I might stand a chance." He'd looked as miserable as a kicked puppy, and still tryng to suppress amusement at her own misreading of Jason's intentions, she'd found herself gravely promising to do what she could to help. Jason brightened—and promptly begged her to partner him to the housewarming party.

"It might put Dolores off the scent if she thought you and I, well, were going out together. Besides, it'll be a damned good evening. Pity to miss it." His eyes pleaded with her. "Look, if you honestly hate it, you can slip away early. Just be a love and make the grand entrance with me. I'll put it right with your father if that's worrying you."

It was—that and the necessity to stay

clear of Paul Burford. But, reluctantly, she'd agreed to go.

Now, looking into Tania's eager face, her promise to help Jason was clear in her mind. She said carefully, "How about bringing some samples of your work round this evening? I'll show you my rough draft and we can discuss all the details. You could stay and have supper with Dad and me," she added casually, not even daring to think of Dad's reaction to anyone from Kelrozen sitting down at his table.

"I'd love to," Tania said eagerly.

And Dolores, apparently appreciative of Ros' attempts to take Tania's mind off the storm, nodded benevolent approval.

The storm returned in the night wreaking havoc round the village before it finally swung away. Auntie Vi called next morning, to relate a whole series of disaster stories—the worst being the village hall which had been practically demolished when an old ash tree, dislodged by gushing water that had undermined its roots, had crashed down on the roof. "And the flower show and the fête still to come," Auntie Vi had wailed. "I don't know what we'll do."

But Ros' thoughts weren't on fêtes and flower shows as she drove carefully to Falmouth next afternoon through lanes made treacherous by debris and surface water pouring from the soaked fields. She was thinking pleasurably of the satisfactory way the previous evening had turned out.

Her father had frowned when she told him about Tania's impending visit but Tania had soon won him over. Ros realised that Tania had in some ways reminded him of Gwen, whom he still missed very much. She had a shy, quiet, undemanding presence and an eagerness to please that refused to waver under his initial suspicious greeting. What's more, the typing examples she'd brought were impeccable. Ros was impressed and had no hesitation in handing over her precious manuscript into Tania's care.

Jason had called, as though by accident, as they were sitting over the remnants of their meal. And any niggling doubts Ros had felt about interfering in Dolores' grand plan for Tania, were dispelled when she saw the radiant smile Tania bestowed on him. She'd suggested a stroll down to the Waterman's Arms and, after a little while in the crowded bar, she'd tactfully excused herself. They were so deep in conversation that they'd hardly noticed her leave.

Falmouth's streets were busy with holidaymakers. Would any of them want to waste good holiday time coming to buy a book she'd specially signed? How ghastly if no one came at all! When she eventually made her way to the shop that displayed pyramids of her books in its windows, she didn't know whether to be excited or terrified.

She took a deep breath and went in to the effusive welcome of the manager and, blessed relief, one or two people already hovering to have their books signed.

Time passed quickly. The shop made enough sales to broaden the manager's smile and people kindly stopped to chat when there was a lull. She was surreptitiously glancing at her watch towards the end of the session when another book was plonked down on the desk in front of her.

She looked up, astounded, into Paul Burford's face.

"What are you doing here?" she burst out.

"Like the bad penny I keep turning up," he grinned.

"I thought you were in Bristol or Bradford or somewhere."

"Plymouth this week," he said. He leaned over the desk and added in a confidential whisper, "Near enough to slip away and pay a call on our Famous Author —and I'm sure she's as delighted to see me as I am to see her."

She gave that statement the chilly reception it deserved.

"I've already signed one book for you."

"This is for my mother. Her name's Tessa if you'd like to include it in the dedication."

She scribbled the name and her own and silently handed the book back to him.

"She'll be in England—at Kelrozen I hope—for her birthday. She's a great reader. She'll be thrilled with this."

"I hope so," she said politely.

"You must meet her. I'm sure you'd get on well. She's not a bit like me, you see."

Her mouth twitched.

"Ah," he said, "is that the beginnings of a smile?"

"No," she said firmly.

He stood there, tall, smiling, unmovable. "Your time's up here, isn't it? How about me taking you for tea?"

She opened her mouth to refuse, but the manager, hovering within earshot, let her down by thanking her profusely and assuring her that she deserved refreshment after such a successful afternoon.

Reluctantly she gathered up her bag. Half of her mind informed her that she was thirsty after all that talking and smiling and tea was just what she needed. The other half made squeaks of protest while her legs, willing and traitorous, carried her out of the shop.

Paul tucked his hand under her elbow and steered her to a small café in a quiet street.

"A favourite haunt of mine," he said as they took their seats at a table laid with a lace cloth and pretty china. "They do the most marvellous home-made cakes. And talking of marvels," he said solemnly, "you look good enough to eat today."

A sneaky little dart of pleasure attacked

her defences because she had taken a great deal of trouble over her appearance. Her curly hair was shining, almond-green shirt-waister crisp and fresh. But all she said was, "I could hardly turn up to sign books in any old tat!"

"Couldn't you? I thought Famous Authors were a law unto themselves."

"I do wish you'd stop calling me that," she said tartly. "I'm not at all famous."

"You will be," he said, in a voice that brooked no argument.

She applied herself to choosing one of the diet-defying cakes that the waitress placed in front of them and turned the conversation to safer topics. She told him of the storm and the wrecking of the village hall. He talked to her of heated board meetings about the changes he was making in the company, but how he was slowly getting things to his liking. "And you might be interested to know that giving Langley the boot was my first real success," he said quietly, "even though we had to save his face by calling it early retirement."

"It would be hypocritical to say that I'm sorry."

"Will you pass the news on to your father? I'd like to think he might come round to believing eventually that I'm not the black-hearted villain he imagines me to be." He paused, then said softly, "You, too, Ros."

She carefully licked a scrap of chocolate icing off her finger.

"I thought I'd made it clear," she said evenly, "that I'll make my own judgments."

"Without being prejudiced by the past?"

"Of course."

"Not so easy, though, is it?" he said, and under the mocking lightness of his tone she caught a trace of another emotion that brought her glance up unwillingly to meet his as he went on, "Whatever has happened in the past inevitably colours the future."

"You learn from experience, true."

"And if that experience is a bad one? Doesn't that make you less trusting? More cynical about other people's motives?"

The bleakness in his eyes caught at her. She had the sudden conviction that he was not so much talking about her but himself, of his own hurt and disillusion. About a girl he'd loved and irretrievably and painfully lost.

She chose her words with care, wishing she didn't have this foolish and irritating urge to put her arms round him and comfort him, as though he were a small boy who'd taken a tumble and needed to be picked up, dusted down and hugged better.

"Perhaps becoming less trusting isn't such a bad idea," she said. "It stops us from making shallow judgments. It gives us the incentive to look beneath the image people show to the world and search for the worth—or otherwise—underneath."

"That's the positive aspect. The negative way—bitterness, introspection, self-pity—seems easier sometimes." Then after a moment he shrugged, smiled wryly and his light mocking words shattered the sympathetic silence that had seemed to enfold them. "Dear me, how did we get on such deep philosophical topics?"

"Your fault entirely," she said, busying herself pouring tea.

He was still intent on treading dangerous ground, though.

"Have you been down to Jago's yard recently?"

"Don't you mean Burford's yard? And no, I haven't."

"I'm keeping to the name everybody knows." He helped himself to a sticky bun and tucked into it with enthusiasm. "I'm pleased with the way it's going."

"If you're pleased, that's all that matters isn't it?" she said brightly.

"Oho! Such biting sarcasm." He clutched his chest theatrically. "I'm cut to the quick."

"Do stop it," she said. "You're scattering crumbs everywhere." Then, sighing because she realised he wouldn't let the matter rest until she'd given him a straight answer, she said, "I don't need to go down to the yard to know how it's progressing. I have a blow-by-blow account every time I see Jason."

"I'm glad he's keeping you in the picture." Paul toyed with his cup. "But I'd still like to know if you approved of the development—of the idea behind it, at least."

She didn't answer right away. She thought

148

of her father who refused to believe anything good would come of the scheme. She thought of Jason who was so carried away with enthusiasm he couldn't believe it would bring anything but good to the village. She thought briefly of her childhood in Pengara, and of the changes she'd seen in her own lifetime.

Then she said carefully, "When I was a child here the village was full of youngsters. Now there are so few that five years ago they had to close the village school. There's very little work around here for young couples—and property is now so expensive that they can't afford to buy houses here anyway. Cottages are snapped up by people wanting to retire here—or as holiday homes that are kept shut up for most of the year." She met his gaze frankly. "Anything that reverses that trend has my approval. And your idea—of flats with small workshops and studios attached to attract craftsmen and artists—might just work. I do have one suggestion, though."

"Fire away," he said.

"You're planning to sell them off as individual units, I gather."

He nodded, watching her intently.

"Would it be a viable proposition to reserve a couple of the units to rent cheaply to young local people? To stop the drift away from the village?"

"People like yourself, you mean?"

She shook her head vigorously. "There'll always be people like me who have to get away—whose horizons need to be wider." Even as she spoke she wondered if that driving urgency was as strong or as heady as it used to be. But she went on forcefully, knowing she was right because it had happened to school friends. "There are plenty of people who've been forced to move because there was nothing for them here and who would dearly like to return."

"I don't blame them," he said quietly. "Pengara's a place that makes you want to put roots down."

"So you'll think about it?"

"I will. And thanks, Ros."

She was pleased; and even a little comforted about the loss that had been more her father's than hers but that had been painful all the same.

They finished their tea and went out into the sunshine.

"Are you going to Pengara now?" she asked as they strolled back into the crowded streets.

"No, back to Plymouth."

She stopped in surprise.

"So you really did drive all this way just to get a book signed? But you could have done that any time. At Kelrozen."

"I promised I wouldn't disturb you there, remember?" His hand was still tucked in that familiar way under her elbow. She could feel the warmth of his fingers, each like an indelible imprint on her skin.

"But that's silly," she said, looking up at him into those grey, teasing eyes. "I . . . I wouldn't have minded."

"Wouldn't you?" His other hand, somehow, seemed to have attached itself to her waist. They stood facing each other outside a gaudily cluttered gift shop. "But would you mind if I claimed my reward for coming all this way? If, for instance, I kissed you goodbye?"

"Yes I would!" She meant to sound indignant. Her voice came out instead in

151

a frail whisper. She tried to fix her attention on a smirking china dog in the gift shop window, but Paul's head blocked her view and, anyway, her lids had this dreadfully languid tendency to close as his mouth came closer and closer to hers.

The china dog smirked on unobserved for an unmarked interval of time as Paul claimed his so-called reward.

And in this, she thought with the part of her mind that was still able to function, as in everything else he did, he was very, very thorough.

8

AFTERWARDS she couldn't believe she'd been so foolish to have stood in the centre of crowded Falmouth letting herself be kissed by that . . . that crazy man.

"What could I have been thinking of?" she moaned to herself as she drove with uncharacteristic recklessness back to Pengara. But of course, that was just the trouble. Thought and reason hadn't come into it. It was pure stupidity. And that wasn't the word, either. But it would have to do because she refused to dig deeper into her subconscious and come up with something that might prove even more unsettling.

After Paul had strolled away, why had she gone on standing there wearing a smile as daft as the china dog's? And when Paul turned to wave before he went round the corner, why had she waved back instead of shaking her fist? Which was what she wanted to do when a few seconds later she

153

came to her senses. It had been no use, then, muttering the put-downs she should have used. It was far too late.

"Everything go all right?" her father asked when she got in.

She felt like shouting, "No, it didn't!" but managed in time to amend it to a polite, "Quite well, thanks."

Fortunately Bill was too full of his own tidings to notice that she was perhaps less pleased with her afternoon in Falmouth than she might have been.

"This television company phoned," he said. "Very anxious to contact you."

She was hardly listening as she took the slip of paper he pushed into her hand. It was only when she dialled the number and took in what the brisk voice on the other end was saying, that she came back to reality.

"They want me on that late-night Arts programme," she said in a dazed voice, wandering back into the sitting-room and collapsing on to a chair. "They want to come down here and interview me for a programme on books by new young authors."

"Well, now, there's a thing," Bill said proudly.

She shot him a look from under her lashes. "They may want to include you, too. The theme of the programme is the influences of landscape and background on the writer's work."

"Reckon I never had much influence—you went your own way," he growled. "Stubborn as a young mule."

"And where did I get that from?" she asked, grinning. "That's certainly a gene handed down from the Jagos. Anyway, it's settled. They'll be here next week."

His answer to that was to disappear behind his newspaper with a muttered, "Humph."

All the same—and without the usual prompting—he was off to the village the next morning for a much-needed hair cut. He also, quite by chance, discovered that his favourite shirt had got rather crumpled in the wardrobe and needed laundering—and perhaps while Ros was about it she'd give his best blazer a bit of a press . . .

At least it kept his mind off the Kelrozen housewarming. Though he hadn't protested when Jason had told him he wanted to take Ros, she knew he thought her a traitor for going. She felt a bit that way, too, though when Saturday came round she couldn't suppress a tingle of anticipation when she saw that after the brief unsettled spell the day promised to be a glorious one and the forecast was good.

The dress Lynn had given her was perfect. The low sun angling in at her bedroom window that evening seemed to draw fiery lights of apricot and bronze out of the golden silk which swirled and clung seductively to her curvy figure. The colour was perfect, setting off her rosy-brown tan, somehow making the velvety blue of her eyes under their thick, sweeping lashes, look deeper, almost blue-black.

She wore no jewellery except for a fine gold chain round her neck and two gold-edged combs sweeping back the glossy tangle of her hair from her cheeks.

"Good enough to eat . . ."

Paul's words echoed faintly in her head. The golden girl reflected in the mirror momentarily lost her smile.

"Don't think about him," she lectured her reflection fiercely. "He isn't going to notice you in the sort of crowd that'll be there tonight. Besides, it's Jason who matters. You're only going for his sake. His and Tania's. Once your duty's done you can come straight back home."

"Wow!" Jason exclaimed goggle-eyed as she walked out to the car.

He leapt to open the car door and swept her a deep bow. "Some outfit!"

"You don't look half bad yourself. Very distinguished," Ros laughed. "Evening togs suit you. Dolores can't help but be impressed. Not to mention Tania. Everything going OK in that direction?" she went on as they drove up to Kelrozen.

"Swimmingly, thanks to you." He gave her a grateful glance. "Being able to meet at your place has made a terrific difference."

"It's amazing how many times Tania has had to consult me over the manuscript this week," she said with a twinkle in her eye. "And such a coincidence that you just happen to drop in while she's there."

"Isn't it," he agreed solemnly. "But I hope we won't be bothering you too much in the future. We've got one or two ideas

157

of our own. Like Tania coming to work as a temp in my office while one of our secretaries is on holiday."

"Does Dolores approve?"

"Tania's working on her," he said. "Paul thinks it's a good idea, anyway." Dolores can't object if he doesn't."

She was glad for Jason. But what about Paul? It was a question she couldn't ask. Jason was so full of himself, so pleased. She could give his answer, anyway. "All's fair in love and war, Ros!" Sure. Everyone knew that. But Paul had been badly hurt once. She knew from her own experience that having someone you love crunch that love underfoot on the way to the next big attraction was tough to live with. If it happened a second time? Despite the warmth of the evening, she shivered as if a cold draught had touched her bare shoulders.

Ros could smell the fragrance of roses as she walked up the steps to Kelrozen's open front door on Jason's arm, and they both stopped in amazement when they saw the transformation that had overtaken the hall. It had been turned into a rose bower. Great swathes of pink and apricot and white hung round the walls, arched over the doors, wreathed up the banisters of the elegant staircase, entwined themselves up several artfully placed pillars that concealed the kitchen door, from which smiling girls in printed dresses and mob caps emerged bearing trays of brimming glasses.

"I see you're rendered speechless." Paul moved over to them as they stood taking it all in. "Dolores does everything with commendable thoroughness. I'm just glad I put my foot down over the Ancient Rome idea, or she would have had me welcoming my guests in a toga and laurel wreath."

Ros heard Jason laugh and fall into easy conversation with Paul. She continued to gaze, suddenly desperate, at the people milling in the hall, her hand still clinging to Jason's arm as though she feared to let go. She didn't want to look at Paul. She wished some other guests had followed them in to distract his attention so that she could slip past him unnoticed and unnoticing.

But Dolores, magnificent in magenta, and Tania, ethereal in fondant-pink, came over to greet them, too, and she couldn't stand apart goggling at the scenery. She had to turn, say something complimentary to Dolores, smile at Tania and reluctantly raise her eyes to meet Paul's.

She meant it to be no more than a quick glance, her face suitably composed into a polite guest-like expression.

Had he been watching her like that since she'd walked into his house, she wondered? As though he'd been willing her to look his way? As though this long, intent moment when their eyes locked, when she heard the far away buzz of other people talking, the clink of glasses, the murmur of laughter—all so remote as to be happening on a distant planet—was a secret only the two of them could share?

He was wearing a conventional dinner jacket and black tie, his red hair was already beginning to look a bit tousled and there was a tiny cut on his jaw where he'd nicked himself shaving. He was, after all, just an ordinary man feeling apprehensive about the evening—wanting it to go well, perhaps wondering if giving Dolores a free hand was such a good idea. So why did she have this extraordinary impression that he stood head and shoulders above the other men in the room? That she must, most urgently, reassure him that the décor was theatrical and over the top—but worked splendidly? And that he mustn't worry about the party because under Dolores' expert guidance it was bound to be a success?

". . . and do you approve of my little efforts at the decorating?" Dolores was saying.

Ros jerked her attention back, dispelling the quick mental image of Dolores in one of her flowing scarlet garments standing on a pair of stepladders to paper the ceiling.

"You've made a terrific job of it," she said warmly. "Congratulations."

Dolores beamed. "You are most generous. It is pleasing to have a professional artist to be appreciative of my small talent in these matters."

"A very considerable talent," Ros corrected her. "Tania has told me how hard you've been working."

"The dear child." Dolores' red-tipped white hand rested on her daughter's shoulder. She appealed to Paul. "And we must not forget how Tania has helped, must we?" she said.

"No, indeed," he said. He smiled affectionately. "You've both been absolutely splendid."

"And we must not keep you young people," Dolores said, her fine dark eyes moving with a hint of calculation from Ros to Jason. "You will wish to join in the dancing—and supper is to be served in the marquee remember . . ." She tilted her head graciously in dismissal, gathered Paul and Tania with an imperious gesture and advanced to meet the next guests.

"So far so good," Jason murmured in Ros' ear. "I think Dolores is getting the message."

"What message?" she said absently.

"About you and me, you ninny," Jason said with a chuckle. "What else? Now all we have to do is appear on the dance floor for one or two suitably smoochy numbers —when Dolores is watching of course— and our smokescreen is complete."

She made an effort to pull herself together. All her certainties seemed to have fled. For some stupid reason she felt as though all protection seemed to have been stripped from her nerve ends leaving her aching and defenceless and open to other people's hurt.

"Jason, should we be doing this?" she began uncertainly. "I mean—Paul and Dolores—it seems—oh, I don't know. Wouldn't it be best if we didn't try to pretend?"

He took her hand. "Who's pretending? I've already told you how great you look . . ." He broke off, staring at her face which, despite the glow of her tan, seemed unexpectedly strained, then said, quietly, "Look, Ros, please don't think I wanted you to come with me purely for my own selfish reasons. If you want to know the whole truth—I thought it was crazy to let your father's vendetta over the yard stop you from accepting Paul's invitation tonight. I didn't want you to miss out. So I tried to think up some way I could get you here." He shrugged akwardly. "It seemed a good idea at the time. It still does. It'll be a good party, Ros, I promise you."

"I'm sure it will."

"Don't be cross."

"I'm not. Your intentions were good—if slightly off target."

"How do you mean?" He looked puzzled, but she covered up quickly, not wanting him to realise that it was her ever-growing wariness towards Paul that was at the heart of her reluctance to be in his house.

"This formal sort of do. It isn't really my scene." She managed a smile. "I'm more geared to impromptu get-togethers with bottles of plonk and bangers and crisps."

"Then all you have to do is let me take care of you," he said, promptly. He tucked her hand into the crook of his arm. "We'll forget everything but enjoying ourselves. Come on, let's see what other delights await us. The garden first, I think. We'll be just in time to catch the perfect sunset that Dolores has booked specially."

The sunset was fierily glorious—and so perfectly on cue that it was almost possible to believe that Dolores had stage-managed the whole celestial spectacular. And when the long summer afterglow began to fade, concealed floodlights restored the colour the night was trying to steal.

Ros let the atmosphere take her over. She made herself forget those uneasy moments when she'd first arrived. She and Jason mingled with the crowd indoors. They chatted and laughed with people they knew and many they didn't, danced sedately to the formal trio in the drawing-room and far less sedately to a rustic group who took over and got everyone up for a hilarious bout of country dancing.

Paul was kept busy circulating among his guests. His red hair acted like a warning beacon enabling her to move casually out of his way if she caught a glimpse of it. The knowledge that she was in control of the situation revived her confidence. She began to relax and to enjoy herself; perhaps even more than Jason, who couldn't find any opportunity to get close to Tania. She was taking her duties as co-hostess almost as seriously as her mother and it was only as they were helping themselves from the groaning supper tables in the flower-garlanded marquee that Tania made her way breathlessly towards them.

A big grin spread across Jason's face as Tania smiled up at him, her brown eyes luminous with happiness.

Ros left them to it and slipped outside. She walked slowly across the lawn. The night air was soft and cool as silk and potent with the seaweedy tang from the water at the garden's edge. A huge moon was vying with the floodlighting for attention and as she looked up in admiration she saw the dark shape of an owl cruise silently above her and disappear into a nearby clump of trees.

"Lucky old owl," Paul's voice said softly into her ear.

Her breath caught in her throat. He'd appeared out of the darkness as quietly as any creature intent on a night's hunting.

"Lucky?" she managed lightly. "How do you mean?"

"Able to turn his back on all this." Paul gestured round, at the noise and laughter coming from the marquee, at the strolling couples, at the distant thump of music from the house.

"Aren't you enjoying your own party?"

"It's . . . well, shall we say that it's not quite what I envisioned when I first decided on a housewarming?" His tone held wry amusement. "Dolores rather took it over, I'm afraid, and I hadn't the heart to dampen her enthusiasm. She's thrown her heart and soul into this party, you see, because she believes it's one way she can show her gratitude to me for giving her and Tania these months in Kelrozen. I couldn't hurt her feelings by calling the whole thing off."

"But you wanted to?"

"Well, it has come a long way from my original idea of a few good friends in for dinner," he said drily. "Mind you," he added, moving closer, "I suppose then I'd have missed seeing you looking like a fairy-tale princess straight from the pages of your fantasy world. And that would have been a terrible deprivation."

She took a breathless step away from him, but he caught her hand.

"Don't you feel a mad urge, Rosenwyn Jago, to let the moonlight go to your head? To run with me away from all these people? To go down to the creek and launch a boat and follow the silver path of the moon wherever it leads?"

"If it's Dad's dinghy you're thinking of we wouldn't get very far."

He chuckled. "Will you settle for a sedate stroll around the lawns then, golden lady?"

"Much too awkward in high heels," she said promptly.

By way of an answer he pounced, picked her up and carried her shrieking over the grass.

"Put me down, you oaf!" she ordered, unable to stop laughing.

"Sure," he said, setting her down gently when he came to one of the gravel paths some distance from the house. "Now will madam take a walk with me?"

"Do I have any option?"

"None," he said gravely, "because I can run faster than you and I'm altogether bigger and stronger."

"Not only an oaf but a chauvinist to boot!" But she couldn't hold on to her indignation, particularly as he then proceeded to make her feel totally at ease.

They talked about nothing of any consequence: trivialities, laced with a good helping of nonsense and jokes. But as their steps carried them back towards the lights and the noise she found it was almost a physical effort to wrench her thoughts back to the party, other people . . .

Then suddenly he caught her hand and towed her round to the back of the house.

"Through the kitchens, I think," he said, opening the back door and pulling her through the busy behind-the-scenes bustle. "And up the back stairs."

"Paul, what is this?"

"You'll see. In my study. Here."

In Uncle Pedrek's day this had been one of the cavernous, rarely used guest bedrooms, cold and musty. Now it was a warm and lamplit refuge, the walls lined with books, a couple of comfortable chairs, a large solid desk on which she recognised her own rough draft beside the word processor.

He noticed the direction of her glance.

"Yes, this is where Tania's working on your manuscript."

"You don't mind?"

"My pleasure," he said. "It's doing the world of good for her morale and helping you into the bargain. But this is what I wanted to show you."

There was a large dusty painting propped against the desk.

Ros stared at it in delight. "You've found Rosenwyn Jago!"

"Stuffed behind some old bedsteads in the cellar," he said. "The poor old girl's somewhat the worse for wear I'm afraid."

Ros crouched over the painting and anxiously ran her fingers over the contours of her ancestor's face which floated dimly under layers of dirt.

"I don't think it's as bad as it looks," she said with rising excitement. "The frame's a write-off but the tear can be mended. That dingy brown layer is only discoloured old varnish. It can be cleaned . . ." She broke off with a rueful smile. "Oh, dear. I'm letting my enthusiasm run away with me. I don't suppose you want to be bothered with it."

"On the contrary, I intend to have it restored."

"I don't think it has any commercial value," she cautioned.

"That's not important," he said decisively. "It's the personal aspect that interests me. She's part of the history of this house."

Ros stood up, dusting her hands together.

"It was probably painted by a local jobbing painter."

"Don't worry," he said. "I won't expect to find a Gainsborough underneath the grime."

He moved purposefully to a table in the corner and she smelt the sharp fragrance of coffee as he busied himself with a filter machine.

"I keep going on coffee when I'm working," he said, "and I'm sorely in need of refreshment at this moment. You'll join me, won't you? Or would you prefer something stronger?"

She knew she should go. She knew it was foolish to stay here, the door closed, the curtains drawn against the night, the sounds of the party remote. It was all too underminingly cosy. But she was thrilled by the rediscovery of the picture. It was like finding a much-loved relative alive and well after a long absence. And she was grateful to Paul for resurrecting it.

"Coffee will be fine," she said.

"It'll only take a few moments." He strolled over to where she stood looking critically at her now-framed watercolour sketch that hung, spotlit, on the wall opposite his desk. "Looks good there, doesn't it?"

She shook her head. "It's not one of my best. I can see all its faults far too clearly now."

"Perhaps it reflects your mood at the time?" he said softly. "It's a very down-beat picture. It was a beautifully sunny day, as I remember, yet that sketch seems clouded. Sad."

She was startled by his perception.

"I'd been through . . . well, it had been quite a rough patch," she said. "It was the first painting after a break."

He was standing behind her, so close that she could feel warmth emanating from his body, his breath on her hair. Or was that the oh-so-light touch of gentle caressing fingers?

"Perhaps one day you'll paint me a happier picture."

"One day. Maybe." She sidestepped away from him and began to study the books on the shelves, though afterwards

172

she couldn't remember even one of the titles. The coffee machine hissed and bubbled into a silence she wanted desperately to break.

"I hear you've come to the rescue of the village fête," she said breathlessly.

"It seems a shame to cancel it when there's plenty of room here."

"And what's this about reviving the regatta?"

"Oh, I've been sounding a few people out. If we can get enough support it might be fun to start it up again. Just in a small way. Combine it with the fête, perhaps."

She wished he wouldn't stand there enigmatically smiling, completely relaxed and sure of himself, as he watched her moving along the bookshelves. She wanted to keep a safe distance between them, yet she had the odd feeling that if he kept on looking at her like that her legs would refuse to carry her any further. Her frantic gaze alighted on a cluster of framed photographs.

"These are your parents?" she asked brightly.

"Taken at my sister's wedding in Christchurch last year."

"And this is your sister?" She picked up the photograph. "She's beautiful." The elegantly posed studio portrait showed off the lovely bones, the smooth blonde fall of her hair, the perfect white teeth glimpsed between the smiling pink lips.

"Very beautiful, but she's not my sister," he said, without expression. "Just someone I used to know."

She could have kicked herself then, for the words scrawled across the photograph leapt out at her. *"To my darling, darling, Paul. My love always. Your Chrissie."*

Chrissie? The girl he'd been going to marry?

She replaced the photograph as though it had burned her fingers. It was a moment or two before she could bring herself to glance at him. But he'd moved over to the table in the corner with the now-silent filter machine and was busy pouring coffee.

With his back still to her he said, "I'll be taking Dolores up to London next weekend for a few days. Maybe a week. Her affairs are just about straight now but there are one or two odds and ends to tie up."

"Will she be moving back to London eventually?"

"Probably. Her financial position isn't as bad as was first supposed. Her London friends have lined up one or two suitable properties and I'm going with her to make sure she isn't conned into buying something with dry rot or shaky foundations."

He handed her the mug of coffee.

"Tania's going to be working temporarily at Jason's office, did he tell you?"

She nodded.

"She's taking her responsibilities very seriously," he said, with an amused smile. "Insists she couldn't possibly let Jason down by tripping off to London. Dolores is horrified at the thought of Tania being here on her own, but Tania is a lot more like Dolores than either of them realises. She's developing quite a will of her own."

"Tania's staying here then?"

He nodded. "She'll be fine, of course. But I think Dolores would go with an easier mind if she thought someone sensible was keeping an eye on her." He looked at her pointedly.

"Me, for instance?"

"Nothing heavy," he said quickly. "No more than you're doing at the moment, really. Just being friendly."

She thought uneasily of her involvement with Tania and Jason's budding romance. Would Paul be so keen to ask her if he knew of that?

She couldn't meet his eyes.

"I'm sure Tania would hate to think I was looking over her shoulder," she said reasonably. "If she stays up late or lives on junk food for a week, she won't come to much harm."

He grinned. "True, but . . . well, never mind . . ." For a moment he seemed uncharacteristically abashed. "She's got to stand on her own two feet some time."

That wasn't what he had been going to say, she was sure. A moment later she realised, horridly, that she was right.

He prowled restlessly across the carpet then paused at the desk looking down on the completed pages of her manuscript lying there where Tania had left them.

"You've known Jason a long time, haven't you?"

"Since we were children."

"He seems a good bloke." Was that a hint of doubt in his voice?

"He is." She gulped at the coffee uncaring that it was still scalding hot.

His next question hit below the belt. "Trustworthy would you say?"

She almost choked on the coffee. So he suspected. Of course he would. He was no fool. Had he seen them together? Or merely intercepted one of those radiant glances Tania threw so often at Jason? No wonder he wanted someone to keep an eye on Tania; on both of them.

She pulled herself together. She managed a brilliant smile.

"Jason's been a great help to me since I've been back in Pengara," she said. "He's marvellous with Dad, too." She gulped down the last of the coffee. "And poor Jason will be wondering where I've disappeared to. I really must go and find him."

Paul nodded. He looked suddenly tired. Or maybe it was dejection she saw in his eyes.

She banished the will-weakening urge to comfort him. They had to work the whole thing out between the three of them. She couldn't—mustn't—get involved.

"Thanks for the coffee," she said. She moved briskly across the room, putting space between them, trying to resist the compulsion to look back, but at the door she couldn't help a last, final glance.

He was standing with his back to her, shoulders slumped, staring at her sad little painting on the wall.

The eyes of the laughing girl in the photograph seemed to mock her as she slipped softly from the room.

9

THE television crew descended on the village like a swarm of alien creatures bent on a takeover.

Ros was hustled from location to location under the interested eyes of the village while the interviewer, with the skill of long practice, plied her with questions. Ros breathed a great sigh of relief when it was all over and the gear was loaded into the vans.

"You've done real well," Auntie Vi said proudly as she helped Ros clear up after they'd left. Then, in a stage whisper, "Where's Bill? Is he in a good mood? My dear soul, did you see him preening when they were filming him in the lane outside?"

Ros laughed. "A star is born. And he's upstairs getting changed out of his best bib and tucker. Did you want him for something?"

"Not me. John Pritchard. He's coming round later to sound him out about being on this regatta committee they're setting up."

"Dad? Really? I doubt if he'll accept."

"Don't know about that," Auntie Vi said. "He do look a lot more like his old self lately. Quite perky, in fact."

She began to help Ros carry the dirty cups and glasses left from the onslaught of the television crew into the kitchen.

"He has been trying, true," Ros said thoughtfully.

"It's more than just trying," Auntie Vi said firmly. "He looks a deal better than he did and altogether sharper. And did you know that he'd been down to the yard? No? Well, he didn't tell me, neither. But he was seen only last Friday talking to the builders."

Ros stared at the old lady in amazement.

"Don't go saying nothin' to him, mind! If he wants to keep little secrets, that's all to his benefit, I reckon. Shows his mind's starting to work again," she said with satisfaction.

"If he goes on this committee, it'll mean getting involved with Paul Burford . . ."

"All to the good. It'll maybe bring him properly to his senses. He can't go on

bearing grudges for no good reason."
Auntie Vi's expression softened. "That
young man's setting himself to be a proper
good friend to the village. Letting us use
Kelrozen for the fête—and now he says
that for every pound we raise to repair the
village hall, he'll match it . . . To my
mind, he don't seem a mite stuck up or
pushy or full of fancy city ways."

Ros swooshed hot water round the cups.
"No, he isn't," she agreed quietly.

"Your dad'll find that out for himself if
he d'go on this committee. So it's up to us
to do what we can to persuade him."

Privately Ros thought it was a lost cause,
though when her father came downstairs
and Auntie Vi told him of John Pritchard's
impending visit, she added her own
encouragement to Auntie Vi's.

She was surprised at his reaction. He
put up a token show of grumbles, but he
didn't turn the idea down flat as she'd
expected. He remained thoughtful until
John Pritchard arrived, and his old friend
had scarcely time to recall the regattas
they'd enjoyed in their youth before he
was agreeing that it needed people with

181

their experience to counterbalance the younger element who knew nothing of how things had always been run. It took only a minimum of coaxing before he succumbed.

She thanked John Pritchard warmly when he left. "This is just what Dad needs to start getting him back on his feet."

He looked pleased. "Knowing how Bill's been, I thought it'd be hard going. It's a good job young Burford persuaded me to try."

Paul again. The wretched man's name seemed to crop up far too often for comfort. It was becoming harder by the day to remain objective and unconcerned about him, though she did her best. It was only in those vulnerable moments on the edge of sleep that her mind let slip images that she preferred to forget: Paul laughing, talking, his grey eyes alight with teasing good-humour. Paul looking with warm affection at Tania. Paul, shoulders slumped in dejection, as she slipped back to a party that had become, suddenly, unbearably noisy and garish and from which, seeing Jason and Tania coming indoors from the romantically moonlit garden, faces rapt and scarcely able to take their eyes from each other, she had fled at the first possible opportunity.

She wanted to feel happy for Jason and Tania, but she was haunted by the knowledge that their blossoming romance meant heartache for Paul.

Perhaps when Dolores and Paul had gone to London she would be able to put these silly fancies aside, start to appreciate the good things that were happening: her father's advance towards full recovery, the way the work on the book was rushing ahead, the realisation that it needn't be too long now before she could make plans to return to London.

All such happy prospects. But somehow the elation she should be feeling wasn't there—and that disturbed her even more.

Dolores, having put the party behind her, was now preparing to do her bit for the forthcoming fête and regatta. She cornered Ros as she was leaving the studio one evening to enlist her help.

"I have the idea that we shall have paintings and artful things on display in the hall of the house, and the dining-room where the teas will be served," she declared.

"Artful?" Ros queried faintly.

"The good class ornaments, potteries and so forth." Dolores beamed. "I go to London tomorrow. I have many contacts who will be generous. I shall of course approach local people—like yourself—to be also generous. A picture or two perhaps?"

"Oh . . . er . . . of course," Ros said.

"And if you would be so kind as to help me with the arrangements and the selling on the day?" She flourished a clipboard, poised her pen over it and challenged Ros with a flash of her black eyes. "We have not much time, you understand. Not like other people who have organisation already." Then, before Ros could even open her mouth, she cried, "Thank you a thousand times," scribbled on her clipboard and sailed away.

Ros grinned. Ah, well. Everyone else in the village would be tied up in some way with the day's events. It might be rather fun, for once, to take part in what Gwen had always called the fête worse than death and she could hardly back out now.

Paul and Dolores left for London early the following morning. Tania was just backing the old Mercedes out of the garage when Ros got to the studio.

"You just missed seeing them off," she cried, leaning out of the window. She was pink-cheeked and excited. "Poor mother's convinced I shall starve myself to death or be carried off by a white slave trader in her absence. She still seems to think I'm twelve years old instead of going on twenty! She was throwing advice and instructions at me until Paul practically strong-armed her into the car. He was getting quite exasperated." She giggled happily. "He went off with a face like thunder."

Ros thought sadly that it was more likely the prospect of leaving Tania and Jason with every opportunity to be together that was upsetting Paul, not Dolores' protracted advice to her daughter, but she could hardly put a dampener on Tania's high spirits.

"I'm going into Jason's office," she said importantly. "Officially I don't start until next week, but the secretary who'll be on holiday is showing me the ropes. And I'm getting on well with your manuscript," she called as she drew away. "It won't be long before it's finished."

It was such a glorious morning that it seemed a shame to be indoors. Ros gave in to temptation, grabbed her sketch-book and walked out on to the lawns that sloped to the creek, meaning to search for some wild roses to draw for one of her illustrations for the new book. Instead she found herself drawn to Kelrozen.

She'd always felt a deep affection for the house that had been in her family for so many generations and today, alone in the hot, flower-scented stillness of high summer, the feeling was strong that she only had to stop and listen carefully and she would catch the echo of laughter, hear the soft swish of a silken gown, the murmur of voices, a patter of footsteps on the gravel path, the sound of children's laughter . . .

Her fingers unconsciously tightened on her sketch-book until the knuckles whitened.

A house built for a family. And one day Paul's children would play in these gardens, sail their boats on the creek, squabble and laugh and dream under Kelrozen's sturdy, sheltering roof, while Paul watched over them with love and understanding and pride.

And she, Ros, would be far away, living the life she had so carefully mapped out for herself following her profession and pursuing an independence that her experience with Malcolm had warned her was the only way to achieve any sort of harmony in her life.

She stared blindly at a stone urn of geraniums. She had a funny, uncertain feeling when she thought of Malcolm these days—like looking at an old faded photograph that wouldn't quite come into focus. Try as she might, it was hard to recall the elation she'd felt whenever she was with him, as though it had all happened a long time ago to someone else.

A tear slid down her cheek, startling her. She scuffed it away with an impatient hand. She hardly ever allowed herself to cry, however hurt or angry or frightened she was inside. And everything was looking so rosy now—Dad getting better, her career on the up-and-up.

She gulped and sniffed. It made no difference. The tears welled up inexorably and suddenly she was too tired to fight them back. She slumped down on to the warm, dry grass, and buried her face in her hands, and it seemed she was weeping for past loneliness and disappointments, for recent anguish when Dad was so ill and Malcolm had let her down.

She let the tears flow until there were no more, then she scrummaged for a tissue in the pocket of her denim skirt, mopped her eyes and blew her nose.

Distant gulls mocked her with their plaintive cries, but the soporific buzz of bees pillaging the flower beds soothed the edges of that sudden bout of raw emotional release.

She felt a sense of relief, as though the tears had been waiting a long time for her to let them go. And now she was cleansed, rejuvenated, empty, like a clean sheet of paper waiting for the first strokes of a brush to shape a new picture from random dabs of colour.

And the picture that formed was one she instantly tried to erase. She wouldn't let him be there in her head lazily smiling his teasing smile, his red hair aflame! Paul!

She gritted her teeth and willed the unwanted picture away, but like the man himself it was tantalising and tenacious. And the implications of this audacious haunting made her clench her fists so tightly that her nails left imprints on her skin.

She wouldn't be attracted to him! She wouldn't think one more time of the turbulent emotions aroused when he'd kissed her, or of those delicious light-hearted moments out in the moonlit garden on the night of the party. They meant nothing to her and certainly nothing to him.

It was no use. With a sense of fatalism she let her mind accept what her heart already knew: that he had come to mean more to her than she was prepared—or wanted—to accept. That try as she might to deny it, she was irresistibly attracted to him.

Infatuation. That was the word. She might think it to be something deeper. Might, in some secret part of herself, want it to be. But she knew that was the way to more hurt, more desolation. Better to acknowledge the weakness now. That was the first step to overcoming it, conquering it.

Her life was her painting, her books, her future in London. It didn't include Paul Burford; couldn't include him. She had to get that firmly into her head. It was Tania he wanted. Innocent, pretty Tania who had fallen for someone else and seemed oblivious to the hurt she was causing.

Ros hugged her knees, her gaze trailing absently over the curlicues of wrought-iron work on the conservatory. Paul had enjoyed teasing her. That was his way. A jokey, lighthearted way which he used to cover his basic kindness and generosity.

And kind and generous he was. No doubt of that. Despite all her earlier—and justifiable—misgivings she could no longer deny that. A man with the kind of inbuilt confident charm that was particularly dangerous to someone on the rebound who might conceivably read into it far more than was intended. As she was so foolishly beginning to do.

She picked up her sketch pad, selected a pencil from the handful in her pocket.

Thank heaven she'd seen the warning signals in time. She could now deal with the whole silly business before too much damage was done.

She concentrated her attention firmly on the house. The first thing to get out of her system was Kelrozen itself. She was getting far too nostalgic and moony about it, so while she had the chance of the place to herself, she'd jolly well sketch and paint it until she was bored and fed up with trying to get every stick and stone on paper.

Then she'd give the paintings to Dolores to sell at the fête—and hope that each one that sold would take a piece of her idiotic fancies about the house and its red-headed owner with it.

The morning after she returned from London with Paul, Dolores summoned Ros to Kelrozen. The breeze of the last couple of days was throwing its weight about prior to turning into a full-scale gale. Ros was practically blown round the garage block in a confetti shower of petals torn from the overblown roses and a whirlwind of dust attacked her as she scurried up to the house.

She closed her eyes too late. Something gritty and sharp lodged under her eyelid. Streaming tears she groped her way through the conservatory entrance and bumped straight into Paul.

"I must go away more often if this is the greeting I get when I return," he laughed as she fell into his arms. He steadied her, then said sharply as he realised her distress, "Turn your face to the light. Let me look."

He gently and firmly examined her eye and defty whipped out the offending piece of grit with the corner of a clean hanky. "Better?"

She blinked cautiously and nodded.

"Fine."

She still saw him through a blurry veil of tears. Perhaps that was as well. She'd worked hard at convincing herself that she was facing up to her silly infatuation in a thoroughly practical and sensible manner, and she'd been sure she was winning.

But the touch of his fingers on her cheeks, the warm closeness of him as he bent over her, almost demolished her defences before she'd had chance to test them out properly. Try as she might to stay calm, her pulse rate zoomed upwards, as though her blood was cartwheeling through her veins.

With an enormous effort she took a step away from him. "Thanks for the first aid," she said lightly. "Quite the boy scout."

Panic gave her voice an uncharacteristically acid edge.

"You're feeling all right, are you?" He sounded puzzled. "Not dizzy or anything? It's nasty getting something in your eye."

"I told you. I'm fine." She turned away. "Don't let me keep you."

"I was only going down to Jago's to see how work's progressed while I've been away." Rain spattered suddenly against the glass. "There's no rush. I can wait until the shower's over."

"Dolores is expecting me."

"Don't go! Sit down, Ros." There was urgency in his tone. "Just for a minute. I want to talk to you."

But she didn't sit down. She didn't even look round. She merely said in an impatient way, as though she were being kept from attending to other, more pressing, matters, "Is it important?"

"To me it is," he said in a low voice. "I have to ask you, I'm sorry, Ros. About Jason. And Tania . . ."

"No!" The cry burst from her.

She was horrified. She didn't want to be the one to spell it out to him. To see his hurt would be like having a knife plunged into her own heart.

"He's buying an old barn, isn't he? Converting it to a house?" His voice was expressionless. Relentless. "Did you know that?"

A couple of evenings ago Tania and Jason had insisted on taking her to see the barn and the scrubby piece of land Jason was negotiating to buy. They'd been like a couple of children unable to contain their excitement. Wanting to show it all off. Not seeing brambles and tumbled masonry and sagging beams but the house and the tamed garden that would one day stand there. Even the dimmest onlooker might have guessed that here were two young people sharing secret, delightful dreams.

"Yes," she whispered. "Yes, I know

194

. . . He's . . . it's something he's always wanted to do."

He seemed determined to put her on the spot. His next words confirmed her fears. "And Tania? How does she fit into these grand plans of Jason's? It seems to me she's becoming rather . . . involved in them."

Rain cascaded down the windows. The air in the conservatory was calm and scented but she felt as cold as if the rain and wind were sweeping through the massed green plants.

"Then it's Tania you should ask about it," she cried, suddenly cross and upset. "Or Jason. Not me!"

His movements were quick and quiet. He was close behind her before she realised it, his hands on her shoulders, spinning her round.

"Ros, please listen!" There was no trace of mockery in his eyes now. He was in deadly earnest. "You see it's important to me . . ."

"I thought I heard voices!" Dolores' voice echoed down the conservatory.

"Oh hell!" Paul exclaimed between gritted teeth.

"You have been caught in the rain, Ros?" Dolores enquired, invisible at the drawing-room door behind the banks of abundant greenery.

Ros tore herself away from Paul, knowing that in another instant she would have given in to the urge to throw her arms round his neck and hold him tightly and pour out the whole story. And that way she would have betrayed not only herself but Tania and Jason too.

"N. . . no . . ." she stammered. "No, I got here just in time."

"Look, Ros," Paul said urgently, "I'll be back in an hour or so. Will you hang on here? Or better still—could I come down to the studio? We wouldn't be interrupted there. We must talk."

She fought to still the wild beating of her heart, covered her panic with a cool, dismissive smile. "I'm afraid it just isn't convenient today."

"Tomorrow, then."

She shook her head. "It's a bad time."

"In other words mind your own damned business and get lost?" His voice was suddenly cold and flat. "Is that what you're saying?"

It took a great deal of courage for her to raise her head and meet his eyes. They were shadowed and dark and there was a vulnerable look to them that threatened her hard-won control.

She shrugged. "Seems like it."

"Come, Ros!" Dolores called impatiently. "There is much for us to do. We must begin."

"You see how it is—I've hardly a minute to call my own," she said lightly. "I must go."

He didn't answer. He stood there tight-lipped and frowning as she turned from him and walked through the greenery to where Dolores waited impatiently, clipboard in hand.

Her heart seemed as heavy as a lump of lead in her chest. And through her mind echoed the grim knowledge that if she valued her peace of mind she must make darned sure that she kept out of Paul's way until she'd shaken the dust of Pengara from her feet.

10

ROS was so shaken by that fraught encounter with Paul that she could hardly concentrate on paintings and bric-a-brac, but she gradually calmed down enough to congratulate Dolores on the amount and quality of saleable pieces she'd collected and to make one or two pertinent suggestions about displaying them.

Dolores was in an expansive mood. She insisted Ros stay for coffee and poured into her unwilling ears a detailed account of her few days in London into which Paul's name cropped up with uncomfortable regularity.

"Without his aid," she declared, "I should never have found this big house which is converting to four flats—so close to good shopping and theatres. Things I have much missed." She lowered her voice, confidentially. "Dear Paul. For my Tania I could not wish for anyone more kind or considerate." She arched her eyebrows. "I expect you have noticed, yes? My Tania blossoms as only a woman in love can. It is but a matter of time before they declare themselves."

Ros kept her face rigidly composed. Fortunately, with Dolores in full flow, she had no need to speak, merely to nod or shake her head as the occasion demanded. Dolores seemed to take her silence for that of a keen and receptive listener. Her voice flowed on, eventually becoming wistful as she went on from present felicities and launched into reminiscences of the stormy courtship of herself and her late husband.

"He was but a poor student I met when I was touring Europe with my grand-mother. Ah, such a scandal! My family was rich—aristocrats in my own country, you understand, landowners with large estates, and I their only child. They could not comprehend why I should wish to marry a penniless nobody. When I did so against their orders, they disowned me. It was only when Tania was born that we became reconciled."

She sighed heavily. "Tania would have been a considerable heiress in her own right had not fate so horribly intervened."

Her voice throbbed with emotion as she added finally, "If a love comes into your life that is so strong and true, then you are indeed lucky and must never falter for such a chance rarely comes again. I had such luck and I thank my fates for it. And I look forward to the years when I may relive my own happiness through Tania and Paul."

They were words that brought no comfort at all to Ros. That night she lay awake, tossing and turning. Bitter-sweet memories of Paul circled endlessly in her head and she felt so washed out when she crawled out of bed, having hardly slept, that she knew that even if she went into the studio she was incapable of any sort of creativity.

Rain battered against the bedroom window. She pulled back the curtain and stared gritty-eyed at the foamy grey waters of the creek. They reflected her own inner turmoil and suddenly she was tired of struggling with it.

"You're going to London?" Bill was flabbergasted when he came downstairs and found her packed and ready. "Bit sudden, isn't it? And is it to be for long?"

"Just for a couple of days," she said brightly. "I need to check some odds and ends with my publishers." It wasn't quite a fib. She would take all her completed illustrations in to them. But she avoided her father's eyes.

He stuck his jaw out belligerently. "This hasn't got anything to do with young Jason, has it? You've been going round looking as though you've lost a shilling and found sixpence just lately and if I thought it was because he'd let you down now he's lost his head over that Tania . . ."

"Dad! No! It's nothing to do with Jason. He's a good friend, always has been, but that's all."

"Well, something's bothering you, that's clear," he persisted. "Someone in London, then. That it?"

She was startled into silence. She hoped she wasn't blushing. Dad was certainly getting better—all his old sharpness was coming back. She'd have to watch her step. If he found out it was Paul who was the cause of her flight, he'd go bananas.

Before she could frame a suitable answer he gave her a broad wink. "Well, I've never been a one for prying and I'm not going to start now. You just sort it out, girl—and come back looking a bit livelier, eh? And don't worry about me. I've got plenty to keep me busy with this regatta to get sorted."

In the end she stayed four days at the flat. The girls welcomed her as warmly as ever, the publishers were ecstatic about the paintings and her editor took her out to a slap-up lunch. She'd have been fine if each time she glimpsed a beacon of red hair in a crowd her heart didn't do somersaults; if, when she walked down busy pavements, she could stop herself remembering strolling with Paul through Falmouth's thronged streets . . . and that kiss . . .

On the third evening her television interview went out. The programme had hardly finished when the phone rang. Susie slurped more celebratory wine into glasses and went to answer it as the others showered congratulations on to Ros' still-quaking shoulders. Susie came back stony-faced. "For you, Ros. Malcolm."

"It's my lucky night! I had no idea you were back in London. I rang Susie to find out where I could contact you." His voice hadn't changed. Smooth and light it flowed over her in a shower of compliments. He'd just caught the programme. He'd no idea that she was doing so well, he did congratulate her. He'd love to see her again.

It must have been the wine that made her lightheaded enough to agree to meet him for a lunchtime drink the following day.

Susie groaned when she knew. "Are you sure you want to take up again with a rat like that?"

Ros listened quietly as Susie dished up the latest hospital gossip on Malcolm and Avril, but on her way to the pub where she had arranged to meet him the following lunchtime she felt even more strongly a sense of rightness about this meeting.

She smiled as she saw him, lithe, dark and handsome, waving from a corner table in the packed bar.

He took her hand and kissed her cheek.

"It's been a long time, Ros," he said,

giving her that slow, considered, disarming glance that had always turned her knees to water. "Far, far too long for me."

A glass of tomato juice clinking with ice and a plate of roast beef sandwiches already waited for her.

"Clever you, remembering what I like," she said lightly.

"How could I forget?" he breathed. "And seeing you last night on the box. Well . . . you looked so terrific. And I'd no idea . . . that is, I always *knew* you were talented of course, but I've just been into that little bookshop round the corner and there were your books by themselves on a special display stand. You must be absolutely delighted."

"I am," she agreed, sipping her tomato juice. Then she added, sweetly, "How's Avril?"

"Avril?" he said vaguely, as though he found difficulty in recalling the name. "Oh . . . she's fine . . ."

"You're engaged, I hear. Congratulations."

He looked faintly peeved. "Thanks."

"When's the wedding?"

"Nothing's decided yet," he said quickly. "In fact . . . well, actually, Ros, things aren't quite working out . . ." He looked deeply and meaningfully into her eyes, a look which she found now had no effect on her whatsoever. "It's about that —about you and me—that I want to talk about. I've missed you . . . seeing you last night made me wonder . . ."

"If you'd backed the wrong horse?"

"What? What do you mean?"

"Oh, come off it Malcolm, you know perfectly well." She stared at him, willing herself to feel even an echo of the excitement he'd always roused in her. But all she could feel was a pang of sympathy for poor Avril. Had he always looked so self-important and smug? How blind, how lacking in judgment she had been. "You're not getting what you want out of Avril's daddy. He isn't going to give you the nice plum job in his fast food chain that you were hoping for, is he? So it's back to good old doting Ros who, surprise, surprise, seems to be making a name for herself." She grinned. "You're not eating. These sandwiches are great."

"How did you . . ? Oh, Susie, I

suppose," he said sourly. "And it isn't quite like that. I thought we could pick up the threads . . ."

"I'm not a cast-off sock that needs darning!"

The coaxing softness left his voice. His eyes glinted nastily. "You've changed Ros. All this publicity is making you big-headed, I suppose. Well, if you've no time for old friends . . ."

"For old friends, yes," she said amiably. "For you, Malcolm?" She wiped her fingers on the paper serviette and held out her hand. "Well, shall we say goodbye and leave it at that?"

She walked out of the pub like a prisoner liberated after months of confinement. It was over. Truly. She'd felt that the moment she'd heard his smoothly practised line of patter on the phone, but she'd had to meet the cheating, two-timing louse face-to-face to make sure.

There was only her infatuation for Paul Burford now that stood between her and perfect peace of mind. She got into her car and slammed the door shut. She felt confident and in control. Fate had kindly allowed her to tie up one loose end in her life. There was no reason to suppose that, with calm commonsense and composure, she couldn't deal equally satisfactorily with the other.

She'd so built herself up to the idea of facing up to Paul when she returned to Pengara that it was something of an anti-climax to find he wasn't even in the country.

"Gone abroad on business," her father muttered, sorting through papers and files spread out on the table. "With the regatta only a couple of weeks away, too. Made me a lot extra work. Blasted nuisance . . ." But there was no venom in his voice. Despite his grumbles, Ros was pleased to see that he looked cheerful and absorbed.

It was Tania who put her in the picture when she came round that evening with the completed manuscript after Bill had gone off to a meeting.

"That's terrific," Ros said, leafing through the immaculate pages. "Absolutely perfect. Now I've only a couple more illustrations to complete and the book's finished."

"Can't stop long," Tania said breathlessly. "I'm meeting Jason at the Waterman's . . ." Then she broke off, wriggling uncomfortably in the chair. "But there was something I wanted to talk about—it's a . . . a bit embarrassing, actually. Paul was so cross—but Jason and I—we didn't think . . . We just assumed . . ."

"What are you on about?" Ros said, mystified.

Tania chewed her lip, then said in a rush, "You and Jason. I mean, you're not in love with Jason, are you Ros?"

"Me? Good heavens, no!"

Tania searched her face with anxious eyes, then relaxed and beamed. "There! That's just what we told Paul!"

Ros frowned. "What's he got to do with this?"

"Oh, he'd got this silly notion in his head that you were harbouring a secret passion for Jason," Tania said with a giggle, "and that Jason was being an absolute wimp and two-timing you with me. If you see what I mean. He was really uptight."

A lot of clicking seemed to be going on

in Ros' head, as though bits of a jigsaw puzzle were falling rapidly into place.

"Paul thought that—but I thought he—"

"Oh, it was all absolute chaos at the time—what with Chrissie phoning and Paul having to rush off. He'd been looking perfectly thunderous—but I'd no idea why until he turned up in Truro and confronted me and Jason before he flew off on his mercy errand to Switzerland. He said he'd tried to talk to you about it—and you'd got all evasive and upset. But it can't have been about that, can it?"

Through Tania's excited jumble of words she picked out the one fact that coincided with the conversations she'd had with Paul. He'd been trying to warn her, gently, about Jason's feelings—not pump her about Tania's involvement. Her own crazy imagination had put a totally different angle on the confrontation.

"Tania," Ros interrupted, "did Paul know about you and Jason? From the beginning?"

"He caught on pretty quickly," Tania admitted. "And once he did he was a real poppet—keeping mother off the scent, for one. He's been just like the older brother I never had." Her elfin face curved into a mischievous smile. "And he really did put on his big brother act when he put us on the spot about you—looking at me as though I was a tiresome little sister who'd got to be put firmly in her place."

Ros' thoughts were in chaos. And out of the chaos came the giddy, glowing realisation that they'd been at cross purposes all along. Paul was no more in love with Tania than she, Ros, was with Jason!

It was all a foolish misunderstanding. He'd been worried about her—just as she'd been worried about him. And that knowledge alone was enough to put a whole new perspective on their relationship.

Exhileration collapsed as abruptly as it had arisen. Tania was chattering on, her words like shards of sharp glass.

". . . I think he wanted to get everything cleared up before he dashed off to meet Chrissie. She's the girl he was engaged to but she married someone else, remember? Well, her marriage was a disaster from the start, apparently, and she'd taken herself off to Europe to recover from the break up. She'd had her money and her passport stolen in Switzerland. She was in a dreadful state—and Paul was the only contact she had in Europe."

"So he's played the knight errant and gone off to her rescue?" She was surprised how calm and normal her voice sounded.

"He'd planned to go to Belgium on business, anyway, so he decided to take in Switzerland as well." Tania smiled dreamily. "The two of them are together in the mountains right now . . . rediscovering each other—incredibly romantic, don't you think?"

Ros didn't sleep much that night and when she did doze off it was to fitful dreams of climbing through snow and ice up a craggy slope. Her heavy feet slipped and slithered. She had to catch up with the man who strode ahead. She knew it was Paul, but when he turned round it was Malcolm smiling treacherously. Paul's Chrissie strode past, calling, "Sorry, you'll have to go back if you can't keep up with us," and she laughed cruelly as Ros floundered deeper into the snow.

She awoke in a panic, and the cold in her bones wasn't merely because she'd kicked off the bedclothes.

In the following days she began to wind up her affairs in Pengara. She finished the last of her drawings, cleared the studio, and helped Dolores to sort and price pottery and paintings for the fête.

The August sunshine had a mellow feel to it now and at night a huge golden harvest moon hung over the hills. Busy as she was, Ros felt she was somehow marking time. She was haunted by a sadness and emptiness she put down firmly to having the book off her hands at last, to the thought of autumn just around the corner.

It didn't help that Dolores went around looking like a storm cloud and regaled Ros with snippets of news about Paul. He was well. Chrissie had been delighted to see him. As he'd found himself so unexpectedly in Switzerland he was taking the opportunity of doing some walking in the Alps.

"It is madness!" Dolores cried. "He is too easy-going. That girl has no right to call upon him the moment she has trouble.

She has tired of her too-hasty marriage and thinks to get her claws into Paul again!"

Try as she might, Ros' imagination kept feeding her pictures of idyllic flower-strewn Alpine pastures, through which Paul and Chrissie strolled hand-in-hand. Or the two of them entwined on some craggy mountain top, or alone on a pine scented forest track.

"I hope they get blistered feet and sunburn," she said fiercely, thumping a price sticker down so hard that she ripped it. Then she sighed and laughed and painstakingly made out another.

The days drifted on. Paul, she heard, had returned to England with Chrissie in tow but was working again in Birmingham where he would stay until the day before the fête. His mother was due to arrive in London then from New Zealand and he would bring her straight down to Pengara.

"And that dreadful Chrissie is coming, too," Dolores hissed, "in time for the festivities." He was apparently spending his spare time showing Chrissie round Shakespeare country and the Cotswolds.

"It should be my Tania up there with him," Dolores moaned. "I tell her she should go. But now she has joined this secretarial bureau in Truro she thinks more of rushing off to all manner of temporary jobs all over the place rather than considering her future."

It was on the tip of Ros' tongue to say that her future (with Jason) was precisely what Tania was thinking of. But she didn't. It was unwise to intervene. Maybe their romance would fizzle out and Dolores could remain in blissful ignorance.

Ros spent the afternoon before the fête setting up the display of paintings and pottery in Kelrozen's hall and dining-room. The house was full of village ladies arranging flowers and setting the dining-room out for the teas that would be on sale.

It was all bustle and organised confusion. Ros didn't allow herself to be distracted. She wanted to be out of the house before Paul returned with his women in tow. All the same, she found herself jumping nervously at the sound of the few male voices in the house, her fingers unaccustomedly clumsy as they sorted through pots and ornaments. But she managed to get away before the Porsche arrived—wishing she didn't have to turn up tomorrow, but knowing she'd have to because she'd promised Dolores.

The cottage was unbearably quiet when she got back. Bill had gone out to supper with John Pritchard to chew over the last-minute details of the regatta. He didn't need her so much now. Her cases lay half-packed around her room, reminding her that she'd only two more days to get through before returning, at last, to London.

She was too edgy to stay in the house. She ran outside, jumped into the car and took the winding lane along the valley and out on to the cliffs. She stayed up there, hunched on the grass, until the salt-scented twilight closed round her, then she got back in the car and drove home.

When she came to where the road skirted Kelrozen's grounds she slowed down. Lights spilled from the windows and the open front door where the Porsche was drawn up.

Like an actor spotlit on a stage, Paul stood lifting cases from the back of the car.

Voices called to him from the house.

She didn't hear them. Figures moved in the doorway. She didn't see them.

She fought to control her breathing, her hands gripping the wheel, her eyes locked on that familiar, red-headed figure.

The empty days were over. He was back. And she knew that however much she tried to fool herself, this moment was the one she'd been living for all these long, lonely waiting days.

Almost as though he sensed her watching, he straightened and looked towards the gate, his red hair glinting in the light, his face unsmiling, his eyes narrowing to focus.

She jammed her foot down on the accelerator. The car roared in protest and zipped away, carrying her from the warmly welcoming lights of Kelrozen and out into the chilly, desolate darkness.

11

THE day of the fête got off to a promising start. Not only was it warm and sunny, but the postman brought a fat letter from Gwen. When Bill opened it his face lit up.

"Well, I'll be blowed!" he grinned. "Your sister Gwen's going to make me a grandad!"

Ros' delight matched his own. The baby was due at the end of February and Gwen hoped that her father would be well enough to make the journey to New York in the spring to see the new baby.

"You will go, won't you, Dad?" Ros urged.

"Try and stop me," he said and went off to relay the good news to Auntie Vi before he set about the serious business of the day—the regatta that would be held on the late afternoon's high tide. It had all worked out most satisfactorily. The regatta would begin as the fête was drawing to a close so visitors could walk down to the creek to watch and then perhaps be enticed to remain for the grand finale to the day's events—the barbecue.

If Ros had any remaining doubts about leaving her father, his reaction to Gwen's letter dispelled them. Maybe there would be times when he'd still feel low, but now he had something to look forward to, to plan for. And that was one important item that had been missing from his life for a long time.

She dawdled in the cottage as long as she dared. The first visitors were already drifting to the marquee, where the fête and regatta would be officially opened by the leader of the local council, as she hurried up Kelrozen's drive. She found herself looking for a blonde laughing girl among the stalls set up around the lawns but nearly tripped in astonishment as she saw her father strolling across the grass with Paul.

They both paced sedately, heads down, hands clasped behind their backs, obviously deep in amicable conversation.

She fled into the house before Paul spotted her and almost cannoned into Dolores and a tall woman in blue slacks and sweater examining Ros' Kelrozen watercolours.

"Ah, there you are," Dolores beamed. "I have to introduce you to Paul's mother, my very dear friend Tessa."

Tessa Burford's hair, though streaked with grey, seemed only slightly less vivid than her son's. She also had the same warm smile.

"I've heard a great deal about you," she said as they shook hands. She hesitated, her gaze sharply observant on Ros' face, then indicated the paintings. "Paul's a great fan of yours. Now I see why."

"He has bought all four!" Dolores cried. "I have put the little red spots on to say they are reserved."

Ros' heart gave an involuntary lurch, her cheeks warmed. They were lively, eye-catching sketches, but what would these two smiling ladies say if they knew of the two pictures she'd kept back for herself because she couldn't bear to part with them? The ones of the house under a tranquil summer sky into both of which the figure of a man had intruded. He'd almost painted himself into the pictures, as though the hand that held the paint brush had been controlled by the force of her emotions rather than by her hand.

On the first he was a far away figure striding with his long, easy lope across the lawn, his red hair glinting in the sun.

He was the focus of the second painting. He leaned one wide shoulder against the conservatory door, arms folded, staring straight out at her with the warm and teasing look that would forever haunt her dreams.

She had wanted to paint Kelrozen out of her system, but she had only succeeded in locking it more firmly into the place in her heart where, like the creek, the hills and the secret valleys and woods that surrounded Pengara, she held the inspiration for her painting. Just as the romantic, ancient legends she'd heard from childhood were the source and heart of the stories she'd written in her books.

She could accept that now. She had been rebelling against the idea all her life, but now she knew that wherever she went part of her would always ache to return here, to her Cornish heritage.

"We are all to take coffee now, before the rush," Dolores announced. "Will you please to join us in the drawing-room, Ros?"

She shook her head quickly. In any other circumstances she would have enjoyed getting to know Tessa Burford whom she'd instinctively liked. But she couldn't bear the thought of witnessing the happy family gathering, of seeing Chrissie and Paul together, of being the outsider.

When they'd gone Ros stood alone in the empty hall, feeling absurdly abandoned. She drifted to the window and stared at the festive scene outside, wishing she could be contemplating a carefree day like everyone else.

Despite the distant sound of voices in the house she felt very much alone. She hugged her elbows close against the chilly ache that seemed to have lodged permanently around her heart.

Then, as though some inner perception was suddenly aroused, she felt a prickle of anticipation, like mental gooseflesh, along her nerves. Before she could move or breathe or hope a voice said softly behind her, "Anyone would think it was raining out there."

She whirled round. "Paul!"

"Or snowing. Or blowing half a gale."

"Sorry?"

"It's a glorious day," he said. "The fête's going to be a roaring success."

"Of course . . ."

"So why, Rosenwyn Jago, do you stand there looking as though you've just heard that there's a hurricane imminent?"

"Was I?" Joy lit her like a beacon, and even if she had told herself to be sensible it wouldn't have done any good. Sense and reason had nothing whatsoever to do with the way she felt at this particular minute. Hastily she clasped her shaking hands behind her back, in case the urge to reach out and touch him got the better of her.

He stared down at her. "Sad thoughts?"

"Just . . . just thoughts. In general."

His eyes held hers. If things hadn't been different she might have read into his expression far more than he intended. That was her trouble. She'd too much imagination for her own good, an imagination that wanted to blot out reality, that urged her to pretend that the elation she felt in her own heart was reflected in his.

"I got your keys and your note."

She'd put the studio keys in an envelope with a polite letter terminating the arrangement.

"Thank you for allowing me to use the room . . ." she began.

"You're leaving Pengara, then?"

"Monday morning."

"Don't," he said.

"What?" she said, startled.

"Don't go."

"What do you mean? The book's finished. Dad's so much better."

"I know," he said, "I've just been talking to him."

She came out of her daze. "I saw you together. You actually looked the best of friends!"

"Perhaps not quite that," Paul said quietly, "but I have hopes. At least he's just accepted the job I've offered him. You can thank yourself for that particular inspiration."

"Me?"

"I've decided to rent half the flat-cum-workshop units to enterprising local young people. But it needs someone from Pengara to set up the scheme and administer it." He smiled with satisfaction. "I can't think of anyone better than Bill Jago to organise it, can you?"

"I don't believe it!" she said faintly. "You're the last person . . . I mean he thinks you're . . ." But did he? He'd actually said very little about Paul recently. Then there'd been those unexplained jaunts to the yard. And on the occasions she'd walked that way herself she'd seen that the development was shaping up in a robustly-built and interesting manner. It wasn't hard now to understand that it might indeed bring new life to the village.

"Before I went away we'd met a few times on the regatta committee, you know," Paul explained gently. "After a bit of initial parrying—just for the look of it, I think—he discovered my ideas weren't a million miles from his own."

It took a full minute for the facts to sink in, then she said simply, "I'm glad, Paul. I always hoped you could be friends. I'll go away with an easier mind now."

He took a step closer to her. She wished he wouldn't. It had a terrible effect on her breathing.

"You're still determined to go then?" he

said softly. "Is there no way I can persuade you to change your mind?"

The drawing-room door burst noisily open. They both turned to see Tania standing there, beckoning urgently.

"Oh, please, you two, do come. Mother's in a terrible tizzy. She insists on talking to you, Paul. I'm afraid we've given her a shock." Despite her words she was aglow with unashamed excitement.

Ros followed in Paul's wake to find Dolores sitting bolt upright and tight-lipped in a chair while Jason paced nervously across the hearthrug and Tessa Burford patted Dolores' arm comfortingly.

"You will tell them, Paul," Dolores said imperiously, "that this is all nonsense. It cannot be."

Tania flew to Jason's side. His arm slid round her waist. From that secure vantage point she held out her left hand to show the cluster of turquoise and pearls on her third finger.

"We're engaged," she breathed tremulously.

"You are not!" Dolores contradicted. "I do not give my permission!"

"Mrs. Partington," Jason began, sounding as nervous as he looked, "we asked your permission out of courtesy—but we don't actually need it, you know. Tania and I plan to get married as soon as we can. We'd like you to be as happy about that as we are."

"Paul! You hear this? Are you not as appalled as I am?"

Paul exchanged a conspiratorially amused look with his mother before crossing to Dolores and taking her hand.

"Dear Dolores," he said calmly, "I'm afraid I'm not at all appalled. In fact I think it's splendid news."

"But you care so much for Tania," Dolores quavered.

"Of course I do," Paul agreed. "She's like a sister to me."

Dolores dragged her hand free and pressed it dramatically to her heart. "I knew it! It is Chrissie! That girl has lured you away from Tania."

Paul chuckled and shook his head. "I'm one of your most faithful admirers, Dolores, but as a matchmaker I have to confess you're no great shakes."

Ros had been watching Dolores carefully. Underneath the display of dramatics, she sensed that the older woman was genuinely shocked and upset by the disclosure. Jason and Tania, so wrapped up in each other as they were, didn't seem to see it.

She went over to Dolores and crouched down by the chair. "I've known Jason all my life," she said quietly. "He's a very responsible young man—very trustworthy and caring."

Dolores shook her head, the fire suddenly going out of her.

"I think to myself he is your friend, not Tania's," she said dolefully. "I have gone around with my eyes shut. Yet I see my Tania blossom, become a grown-up woman, and still I will not allow myself to think it is anyone but Paul who is the cause."

"Remember what you said to me the other day?" Ros said softly. "About not letting the chance of love slip away? I've remembered that, Dolores. And you must remember it too. Because Jason and Tania do love each other. Truly."

Dolores sighed. "It is not what I would have wished."

"Perhaps that is what your parents said, too."

"Ah, but I was different."

"Older? Wiser?"

Dolores said nothing for a moment, then her lips curled in a mischievous smile that was just like Tania's. "I was eighteen and knew nothing at all of the world."

At that moment someone popped a head round the door and announced the opening ceremony was about to begin.

Ros hastily stood up as Dolores rose from the chair, smoothed down the skirt of her dress, then swept over to Tania and Jason, holding out her arms.

"My dear children," she said. "There is no time now, but later we must all celebrate this engagement in the correct style."

It was all hugs and kisses after that and Ros realised that Paul, having heard every word she'd said to Dolores, was now staring at her with a look in his eyes that suddenly took all the use out of her legs.

Without speaking he reached out his hand. Without any volition on her part, her hand rose and slipped into his. Gently he pulled her from the room, Dolores' voice floating to them as they went through the door, ". . . and now I shall turn my thoughts to the wedding, yes?"

Paul smiled down at her. "By this time tomorrow Dolores will have convinced herself that it was all her idea in the first place."

"I'm glad it's all ended happily," she whispered.

"Me too," he said.

"Paul," she began, knowing she had to ask, "you said something in there . . . about Dolores . . . and matchmaking— and where's Chrissie?"

He tugged her gently towards him and kissed the tip of her nose. "North of the Border I shouldn't wonder with the handsome Scots laddie who shares her newly-found passion for globe-trotting."

"But I thought you . . . and Chrissie . . ."

He stared at her gravely. "That was over a long time ago. I merely sorted out her problems then took myself off for a long, lonely hike over a lot of empty Alps to try and forget a girl with sea-blue eyes. I rejoined Chrissie and travelled back with her. She was keen to explore Cornwall but the call of the Highlands became too strong."

"Oh," she said faintly, her head swimming.

She managed only a squeak of protest as he began to tow her steadily up the stairs. "The fête . . ."

"Your fate is upstairs in my study," he said firmly.

She groaned at the dreadful pun.

He laughed and yanked her inside his study and closed the door. "Now," he said grimly. "It's your turn."

"What for?"

"Confessions. I want to know exactly where I stand. Now we've disposed of Jason, so to speak, is there anyone else I should know about? Your father seemed to think there might be someone on your London stamping grounds who was playing havoc with your heartstrings."

"You've been talking about me behind my back," she said indignantly.

"Because, you dear idiot," he growled, "we both love you."

After that, there didn't seem any reason not to tell him about Malcolm. She made it short and sweet. He nodded with satisfaction, then grabbed her none too gently and pulled her close.

She wasn't sure how long the kiss lasted. She had the feeling the fête, the regatta, even the barbecue might have been long over before her eyes opened slowly and reluctantly.

"So, can we begin again from there?" Paul breathed softly into her ear. "Without phantom rivals and enraged papas getting in the way?"

She rubbed her cheek against his chin. She felt like purring. "Mm," she agreed langourously.

She was sure there were a great many more important questions she should be asking, but she and Paul seemed to be communicating perfectly satisfactorily without a word being exchanged.

When she opened her eyes and the study came into focus again after another couple of decades had passed, she thought perhaps she ought to make some attempts at conversation.

"You got Rosenwyn back, then," she said, eyeing the newly-gleaming picture above the fireplace.

"Seems like it," he said, nibbling her earlobe.

"I'm talking about the painting."

"I'd rather talk about you."

"She looks rather fetching up there, doesn't she?"

"Not nearly so fetching as the Rosenwyn Jago I'm holding."

They looked at each other as though neither could bear to look away.

"Your father said you'd lost all your sparkle lately." He grinned. "He should see you now." Then he added, thoughtfully and with relish, "I wonder how he'll take it when I offer to take his stubborn, self-willed and unruly daughter off his hands?"

She aimed a blow at his head with her clenched fist. He caught her hand, kissed it, pulled her close and, sighing happily, she went comfortably back into his arms.

Above them, the first Rosenwyn Jago in her pristine frame stared down from the wall. Her painted lips seemed to smile with pleasure at the sight of the red-headed man kissing, most thoroughly, her namesake. And her dark blue Jago eyes, that had watched so much change in the

232

house that had been built for her, seemed to hold the knowledge of the long, happy years that lay ahead for them both.

THE END